SVAVA JAKOBSDÓTTIR (1930–2004) is widely regarded as one of Iceland's leading modern writers. Born in Iceland, she moved with her family at the age of four to Saskatchewan, where her father served as pastor for an Icelandic Canadian congregation. In 1940 the family moved back to Iceland where she received her secondary education, and she went on to study English and American literature at Smith College in Massachusetts, and Old Norse literature as a graduate student under Gabriel Turville-Petre at Oxford.

As well as writing fiction, she worked at the Icelandic Ministry for Foreign Affairs and at the Icelandic embassy in Stockholm, as a teacher, a journalist, and a producer of radio programmes, and for eight years she served as a member of the Icelandic parliament.

Her first book of short stories (*Twelve Women*) was published in 1965. Much of her writing focuses on the lives of women, and some of the social criticism implicit in her early works can be seen as foreshadowing that of the women's movement.

Translations of her work have been published in a number of languages, including one previous selection in English (*The Lodger and Other Stories*).

OLIVER WATTS lives and works in Edinburgh. This is his first translation of a novel.

Some other books from Norvik Press

GUNNLÖTH'S TALE

by

Svava Jakobsdóttir

Translated from the Icelandic
and with an afterword
by Oliver Watts

Norvik Press
2011

Originally published in Icelandic by Forlagið under the title of *Gunnlaðar saga* (Reykjavík, 1987).

This translation and afterword © Oliver Watts 2011

The translator's moral right to be identified as the translator of the work has been asserted.

A catalogue record for this book is available from the British Library.

ISBN: 978-1-870041-79-9

Norvik Press gratefully acknowledges the generous support of The Icelandic Literature Fund towards the publication of this translation.

The translator acknowledges the help of everyone consulted in the course of his work, in particular that of Kristrún Guðmundsdóttir.

Norvik Press
Department of Scandinavian Studies
University College London
Gower Street
London WC1E 6BT
United Kingdom

Website: www.norvikpress.com
E-mail address: norvik.press@ucl.ac.uk

Managing editors: Sarah Death, Helena Forsås-Scott, Janet Garton, C. Claire Thomson.

Cover illustration: based on *Gundestrupkarret*, Nationalmuseet, Copenhagen.

Layout: Elettra Carbone

Cover design: Elettra Carbone. Thanks to Sarah Death and Reynir Þór Eggertsson for their advice.

Printed in the UK by Lightning Source UK Ltd.

Contents

The aeroplane hurtles along the final stretch of its run-up into the skies. Nothing left to do but await our destination. At which point it strikes me that I've got nothing to read. I've always had reading matter with me on journeys. Most often papers from work which I buried myself in to kill the time. Papers! Work is hardly foremost in my mind right now! I don't even know where they've got to, the papers which I had with me on the outward journey. I feel a hint of unease as I anticipate a three-hour journey spent in a void. It's going to be a long wait. It would be good to have something to take my mind off things. Because Dís isn't my responsibility on this journey. I'm not even sitting next to her. There's nothing for me to do. My handbag is on the floor at my feet. I know there's nothing in it to read, but the old need to be certain about things, to trust in no knowledge unless it's tangible, has started to stir. And I lean down to have a look, as if I believe that some thriller has suddenly materialised inside the bag. But I stop. Don't dare open the bag. Touch it with my foot. Feel what's inside. A thriller? You'll have to be the judge of that. It's not me who's the author. That's Dís, our daughter. Maybe not her, either. So where does it come from, this invention, if it's not the personal business of a confused mind as they believe, the two men who are guarding her? Is it in the air, like oxygen? Is it in the water that quenches thirst? Is it in the earth which nourishes, giving us the strength to struggle on day after day? Might it actually be fire?

Or is it a prisoner like Dís who sits between these two men in the suits in the row of seats across from me? They're dressed alike in dark blue suits, spotted blue shirts and plain blue ties. The clothing is entirely non-distinctive, as if chosen with the intention of disappearing into the crowd. It proves to us that agents of law and order are not devoid of humanity. And yet it would occur to no-one that they were anything other than what they are. The clothes are not sharply pressed to go with a sleek brief case. So they can't disappear in a group of faceless directors on business trips or officials on government business. Still less could they be taken for teachers or journalists or academics. Those sort of people wear unmatched jackets and trousers, as if to show that they're always at the boundary of two worlds, always somehow on the move. No, these men's clothes are slightly crumpled, the shirt collars a little loose around the neck . . . they're just like detectives in an American film, with this humdrum, laid-back look to fool you. And then the cameraman zooms in, and the hawkish, restless eyes show us that nothing gets past them. Guards' eyes. Everybody can see it. They walk tight up against her on their way into the aisle of the aeroplane. One of them a step ahead, the other close behind. Just like in the cinema. The movies have blown their cover. It's hidden from no-one who's there, and they even become a little ridiculous for not having suspected. Realism makes us into caricatures of who we are.

But they weren't acting. That's not the invention I'm talking about. Never has any invention cut me to the bone with its pain like this reality of seeing Dís come on board the aircraft accompanied by these men. The last of the passengers. Everybody else seated. I couldn't put my hands over my eyes or walk out. I couldn't fling this away from me. She looked over at me just once on this walk of hers. Never has any glance caused me such sadness. I know that it will form part of me for as long as I live. It was at once both close by and distant. In it there was a strange gentleness which was directed at me personally, yet it was at the same time so impersonal that the peculiar thought occurred to me that she was about to make arrangements for me, as if in the next instant she would ask some girl, a complete stranger, to take me on as her mother. Then she sat down, her back straight and head held high, and didn't look over at me again. I'm trying to convince myself that she's done this out of consideration for me. We should be grateful to her, I can hear you saying. Until now, we haven't exactly been considered well acquainted with the police. No: you're right. Quite the opposite. It would be almost ridiculous – in an invented story – if we, if a family like ours, were taken into custody! And involved in a journey like this one! But that is the stark, cold reality as you've yet to see with your own eyes when you come to meet us.

And yet I know she feels no shame.

There she sits. I can barely see her without leaning forward in my seat. She looks straight ahead, and her fair hair flows free and alive down onto her shoulders. The mist from a waterfall comes to mind when I see what a contrast it forms with the dark suits. They both have broad shoulders and big torsos and enclose her between them like the walls of a ravine, as if they're scared that otherwise she would flow away . . . or even fly from their clutches. And perhaps their fear is not unfounded. Not only has she laid claim to both arm-rests so that they, these bulky men, have to sit with their hands in their laps, but her elbows are propped on the arm-rests and her slender forearms are raised like wings, the fingers extended as if she really is taking flight. Beyond these graceful flying arms the blue-white haze of the skies can be seen. It's just as if her space is boundless. She is a bird about to burst free of this flying machine and soar out into the fjords. Who can reach her?

I know that there's a narrow mark on her right wrist left behind by her watch, even though I can't see it from here. Unless it's faded away completely. She threw her watch away. Yes, the gold watch with the crystals which we gave her for her birthday. You don't carry time on your outside, she said, and I was so taken aback that I didn't think to ask what she'd done with the watch. Thought to begin with that she'd flushed it down the toilet, but that obviously couldn't be, because they took everything off her before they shut her away. Watches measure fake time and disturb my pulse and my own rhythm. Yes, I'm just repeating what she said. Time is inside you, she said, and it flows there rhythmically like blood. If you listen to the flow of time inside yourself, nothing will ever be too early or too late. Everything will be in harmony and come of its own accord. I didn't make a fuss about the watch later, either. I know it was expensive, of course, but we've never had to worry about money, and then this was something altogether different. Not the usual carelessness which so often irked us because she didn't seem to appreciate what we gave her or did for her. I also started to feel that it was somehow logical for her to throw the watch away. And so I can't tell you with complete certainty when this started. I just know that at that moment, fake time came to a halt.

They say it was on the day she went to the museum.

It's going to be hard going for me to get all of this across. On the phone I never related anything to you except bare facts, and actually I still think of you as if I were speaking to you on the phone. At first I blamed it on the phone. On the phone's limitations. It was really nothing but a slender cord which filled up so quickly with the facts alone. I also have to admit that I had an inkling – and still have – that the truth – or the invention – will strike you like lightning. And I wasn't able to relate it to you on the phone in a controlled, orderly way. Not so that it would be safe. Because the truth is made up of nuances, and until now we haven't reckoned nuances to tell the truth. Neither of us has found their wayward energy a fixed channel, just as if we were always talking over the phone.

But that was all just a cop-out.

The truth is that I couldn't talk about the truth.

But you might be pleased to know that Óli's a thing of the past now. She left him behind and never spoke about him … but what am I saying? Be pleased? As if that makes any difference as things stand now. As if splitting up with Óli weren't the natural thing to do. What can she do for him as things stand now? And wasn't even Óli preferable to this? I think I mentioned it because Óli seems to have vanished from her thoughts. As if she is suddenly free of love . . . or was it a duty . . . or some mysterious obligation . . . or something else? Because she *is* free, even though she's sitting there between them. In a way I can't explain. Have you ever seen a free prisoner? Take a close look at her when she arrives. Look at her with fresh eyes. Then maybe you'll see the same as I do.

And yet I did everything in my power to have her declared not responsible for her actions on the grounds of mental illness. Or mental disturbance, at least. Or temporary imbalance of the mind. And that didn't exactly take much doing. Still, I talked about her as a problem child in all these never-ending interviews with psychiatrist and lawyer. I told them the honest truth. That she'd caused us anxiety and many a sleepless night since she was about twelve or thirteen. That she was gifted academically and got high marks when she applied herself at school, but that that didn't seem to have any motivating effect on her or fire her ambition because she was prone to idling away terms at a time, either devouring any book which wasn't a text book or messing about writing poetry which she sometimes published in the school newspaper, except when she disappeared from home for whole days at a time: she was even away from home overnight, and said she was gathering experience. Getting to know life. Social Services had sometimes brought her home when she was younger. Yes actually, I knew that she used to drink and that she sometimes came home under the influence even though we'd done our best to introduce her to alcohol in a civilised way, but then she seems to have mostly given up drinking, just as she'd given up smoking without being urged to do so as far as we knew. No, she'd never got mixed up in drugs, thank heavens, and I found it disagreeable when they looked at me searchingly, as if weighing up whether I could be so naive that it could have got past me. But when it was looked into, it turned out that I was right. I did tell them about Óli, though. That she'd followed him to Copenhagen and that he was going there solely for drugs, and that she wouldn't leave him no matter what happened. And I said more or less

11

everything you say under those circumstances: that we had no say in what she did, that we'd sent her time after time to summer schools in England or Switzerland, but all to no effect . . . she didn't seem to know what she wanted, or to have any direction . . . you know . . . everything which we've been over so often. But we hadn't been prepared for this, though. She'd never got on the wrong side of the law, or committed a crime or vandalised anything . . . never meddled in politics either, to my knowledge. This was something totally new! And at this point I altered my tone of voice as if everything I'd been saying beforehand was merely a description of a normal modern-day teenager. Something serious must have come over her, I said. This couldn't be normal!

Yes, that's what I said in front of these people who held my daughter's fate in their hands. That she couldn't be normal. Admittedly, I know now that what I said made little difference. After the examinations and investigations they agreed that she wasn't normal, the psychiatrist and the judge. Yes, she's been declared mentally ill. But what was I thinking? About the company and our hope of getting ahead and making more money? About our reputation? Is it less damaging to your reputation to have a child in a mental institution than in prison? Or was I thinking of her physical and emotional well-being? At first I convinced myself that I was. I couldn't let her be locked up like a common criminal! Little Dís! My little Dís! But she always stood firm. Never changed her story. And now everything she said has been judged a fabrication, her truth an innocent invention. No, not even that. Just nonsense.

Do you remember when we got the phone-call from the embassy? It's certainly not so long ago, and most likely your time since it happened has been an empty wait between real, tangible events, as if you're sitting on a bus with your eyes closed, only opening them at bus stops. For me it's been altogether different. It takes quite an effort for me to recall these events. Not because my memory is getting worse or because I'm being dulled by exhaustion or worries or anxiety. Though God knows this has weighed on my mind an awful lot. No, what's going on in my mind is entirely different from when you try to dredge up half-remembered events out of a tired mind. For me it's as if the last stop in fake time, as Dís calls it, has been shifted or moved away and belongs to another time and another space than the one I'm situated in, or used to be situated in – as if I'm coming back from an interminably long journey, which of course I am, but the effort of opening my eyes at these old memory stops looks like it's going to prove difficult for me. I get no useful clues from this endless ocean of air which enfolds me. If I look out of the window, I'm reminded only that right now I'm plunging through the hidden depths of the sky, awesomely beautiful. I even have a dangerous urge to give up remembering and to simply throw my watch away like Dís.

Suddenly the air hostess is standing beside me with a glass on a tray. For one strange moment I feel as if she's about to start

13

serving me the sacrament, standing there in uniform, stooping a little, and silently – with a touch of ceremony – holding out the glass to me. I'm so startled when I've got my bearings that I've nearly started laughing. And yet she has been of help to me. I can tear my thoughts from the depths of the skies outside and continue to remember. I haven't ordered anything, but do you think maybe our guards – Dís's – are offering me this? That goes beyond humanity! It's a courtesy which at the same time is some sort of peace offering. The drink – if accepted – would create some kind of social equality among us; their power would lessen, our freedom increase. They themselves are offering it personally, for they must certainly be paying for it out of their own pocket. I can't imagine that expenses of this sort are covered by the national budget. For a moment I feel almost warm towards them, and out of old habit I'm on the verge of accepting the drink so as not to upset them. But I decline it. I don't actually want anything. It's true! I don't want anything. I haven't felt like anything for the past few days. I've forced nourishment upon myself in order to keep up my strength. I naturally ask myself almost straight off whether I've declined out of bitterness or self-pity – whether I'm putting on a show in front of them and am unwilling to drop the role of the victim's injured mother, though I truly have no need of this in front of Dís. There she sits, majestically almost, a glass of orange juice in one hand, her other elbow still on the armrest, like a princess in a fairy-tale where everything that happens is natural and needs no explanation. I could swear she gives not a thought to who's paying for the drink, as if it went without saying that the drink came flying to her through the agency of these two servants who never leave her side! It isn't arrogance. You know that she's never been arrogant, no matter what might be said about her in other respects. That we've rather told her off for not being particular enough about her friends, and mixing with just anybody. With Óli for example. But it's this far-away look about her, like when she looked at me on the way to her seat on the plane when I thought she was going to start making arrangements for me. I'm no longer . . . the guards aren't . . . in her eyes, no-one seems to be playing their part any longer. We're no longer what we are or what we think we are. I can see it in her, too. She is the perfect free prisoner. A symptom of schizophrenia, some might say. I'll say nothing about that. There's a description of the illness in the pocket of one of the men in suits, of course. It's doubtless called something there, but I don't have a name for it . . . not yet . . . but I'm fully reconciled all of a sudden to having declined the drink for the single simple reason that I didn't want it. Why should I impose things on my body out of consideration for others?

We should have listened to her more carefully.

When I think back to that day we got the phone-call from the embassy, the first thing I hear is a racket, like from a pair of screeching terns. That's us. We're not even listening to each other.

No, to hell with it! I wash my hands of it!

And you stood before me on your way out to a meeting and I looked at your snow-white hands and asked icily just what it was you were going to wash off. I wasn't aware you'd ever got them dirty! And I screeched accusations at you, of being heartless, selfish and God knows what else. But that was just a pretext. The anger which gripped me was so overwhelming because you'd beaten me to it. It's not possible for both parents to wash their hands of it. That just can't happen. And now I couldn't wash mine.

So I have you to thank that I went. Maybe I would have got over it and gone anyway, but my maternal instinct suffered a setback. Yes, my motherly heart was beating sure enough, but how extremely doubtful and weak-willed it was, considering the indomitable organ it's meant to be. It wasn't an organ, it was an electric blender which whipped into a single mixture anxiety about my child, wounded ambition, anger. Because although I had the company's interests to protect no less than you did, I had various other things as well. I was suddenly like a fortress under siege, riddled with bullet-holes.

She must have got involved with criminals . . . maybe she's become a political terrorist . . .

And you said you couldn't go to the meeting! I stared at you dumbfounded. But who am I to talk. And I would have understood perfectly your being unable to go to the meeting if you believed she really *had* become a political terrorist. But as you recall, I thought you'd gone a tiny bit crazy. Because who's ever heard of a political terrorist breaking a display cabinet in a museum and stealing an ancient artefact from it?

Yet maybe you hit the nail on the head. Except that Dís doesn't use the word *steal*. She says . . . yes, I'm sure she used the word *reclaim*. And isn't that exactly what political terrorists say they're doing?

I on the other hand was afraid that she'd been led astray and got mixed up in drugs. That this stray cat, Óli, whom she tracked down time after time to nurse, had finally managed to bring her down. Yes, I thought – led astray: if your children leave the straight and narrow you're all too ready to put it down to impressionability. It never occurred to me to credit her with any initiative, let alone independence.

I thought I wouldn't be able to bear it. I was collapsing. It's so strange that I don't remember having thought of Dís as a person just then. I thought about us as a family. As a whole. She was a part of us. And now it was no longer possible to hide the fact that I didn't have a model child. There was something the matter with my child. Whether it was nature or nurture or both didn't really matter all that much in these first moments of anger and impotence. It certainly preyed on my mind later whether she'd inherited some lack of willpower which prevented her from exploiting her own intelligence – good sense and good fortune are two different things – why though? – but that first day, I thought my way of living was under threat. I knew what people would say. I would be criticised for having let my job come before my home life and my child's upbringing . . . I hadn't given her sufficient love and attention, and so on . . . and at that moment I knew that I had been nursing this worry in my own breast all along, that the words I put in the mouths of others were my own worry that this was the way things would turn out . . . as if I'd known all along that this is how it would turn out and now I wanted to wash my hands of it. Not to drink this cup to the bottom. The one who was meant to demonstrate that I could make a success of everything I turned my hand to, little Dís herself, had let me down!

Weren't you thinking along the same lines when you managed to come out with your vitriol just before I did? For that I'm grateful to you, because it meant I needed to stand up for Dís against you.

At least, I thought at the time that I was standing up for her.

If she's not on drugs, then there's got to be something the matter with her!

You were only too pleased to accept this explanation. And I didn't know at the time that this was the first step of my escape. Nor had it in any way become the conscious strategy which it became later on, with the aim of getting her off punishment. You can understand neither the criminal nor the madman, though the powerlessness of the latter is absolute. And you sympathise with his powerlessness. Become stronger yourself as a result. And so struggle for power, too, is an inherent part of this. We could see this in ourselves, although we avoided discussing it. We ourselves stood at the centre of the pyramid: above us stood acquaintances, clients, contractors, society, the ones who would now start to pity us or look down on us or trip us up. In our case you could even add the governments of two nation states to the list. That's hardly a minor detail. But that didn't trouble me until later. I'm still not sure that we had grasped it at that stage. At least, we said nothing. Still, the suspicion has preyed on my mind that it was registered on our breath. What we *did* both know instinctively though, was that we were strongest in our own home. That's why going to the meeting that evening was more than you could manage, just as it was more than I could manage to talk to a single person before I left for Denmark.

Nor did we speak together much after that. Before I left. We needed a channel. There was a blockage somewhere. The emotions flowed like a river or lake when it's raining, finding haphazard routes as it escapes from itself. The spring which ought to have a safe channel after thousands of years of steady purpose and instinctively knows its course was blocked and fed no tree roots. That's why we didn't know what we were supposed to say, to Dís or to anyone else. I'd even started to pity you for being so wrapped up in the company that you couldn't make it to Denmark with me. I could flee, though. Was it possible to prevent it from getting in the papers? Rumour of it would get around of course, but people can act more like they know nothing if there's nothing about it in the papers. This is embarrassing for other people as well. Just what were people supposed to say to us? It's not exactly the stuff of everyday life in our circle of acquaintance, the kids breaking museum display cabinets in broad daylight with the intention of stealing a prehistoric golden beaker, the like of which isn't to be found anywhere else in the world. To my knowledge, neither is it the stuff of everyday life for them to fall foul of the police, even for lesser misdemeanours. And what were we to have said to such model citizens? You know, if I were an author, I would never make fun of model citizens like us who don't know what they're to say to other model citizens when disgrace befalls them. It's like mocking people who are trying to save themselves from drowning with a mediocre breaststroke because they don't know the butterfly or how to swim underwater. Both the depths and the skies are out of reach for such people.

I made it into the prison on a respectable breast stroke. I had perfect control over how I conducted myself. Yes, I behaved as if – where I came from – stealing ancient artefacts was a part of everyday life among respectable people. Nothing to kick up a fuss about! I had an appointment booked as well, as if I were going to the dentist. Nor was there anything in this prison's entrance or reception which took me by surprise. I'd so often seen something similar in the cinema or on television: a respectable grey-haired warden behind a counter, in a prison guard's uniform but without a cap. There's an almost fatherly gentleness in his expression when he watches me walk in, and the mother, I . . . no, this isn't dramatic enough for the movies. I don't let my feelings get out of hand, and he's immensely relieved about it, this man with the gentle, fatherly expression. He watches me sympathetically, understanding right away that Dís is the object of our common concern and that I'm not going to flare up with accusations against a prison warden or the police about the arrest, ill-treatment, or any of the sort of thing which is thought to spice up the mother's role in the movies. I'll listen to the facts before I pass any judgement. It's plain to see that I'm a rational person, and no-one can see that all of a sudden I've started to weigh many tonnes. I need to put everything I've got into lifting my feet in order to make it these few steps. When I say what I've come for, I realise that the heaviness is in the atmosphere as well. It's so thick that my voice becomes hoarse and what other people are saying barely reaches my ears. The duty-officer's manner reminds me of an actor in a mime when he calls something into the room off to one side and beckons for the warden to come. He's wearing a grey shirt and grey trousers and has a bunch of keys in one hand. I can't believe that this is happening to us – to me, you, and Dís. Then I follow the warden in through a door and along a dim, narrow passageway with sturdy black steel doors and suddenly receive a blow under my ribs so that I can hardly draw breath and I'm no longer me, but pain personified remembering a little new-born baby in her arms. The little miracle's defencelessness causes such piercing sadness that for a moment I wish it will never grow bigger: that my arms could form a magic circle around this life for eternity to shelter it from suffering and protect it from the wickedness of the world. And yet I wish with all my heart that it will grow and thrive and be allowed to live. While I stand behind the warden at the locked steel door and wait for him to put the big heavy key into the lock to let me into the cell where my child is being kept, I feel as if I won't be able to bear this paradox of love which causes me such suffering. I wish that we could swap roles, that I could take upon me this misfortune which she's wandered into because it proved beyond me to ward it off.

The paradox of love, I say.

Is it possible that this could be a flaw in love? Not a paradox?

I don't know why that occurred to me. A flaw in love! Is there such a thing? Doesn't that run counter to the nature of love . . . I mean, isn't there some error in my *logic* here?

And then I'm standing by her and we fall into each other's arms. I hold my arms around her, feel the slender little body slacken in them, I rock her like a baby; we are a closed magic circle and nothing can reach us until she gasps for breath, so tightly do I hold my arms around her, but I don't dare let go because now it seems to me as if I won't survive what follows . . .

She tears herself free and says:

Don't worry, Mum.

It was like she'd smacked me across the face. Don't worry, Mum! Jesus Christ! The gloves are off, already! I'd thought she'd understand now that our warnings and concerns had been justified. I'd been expecting unconditional surrender in this two-man struggle, but now she continued to behave as if my concern for her showed a lack of self-control, bossiness even. In a familiar helplessness over the way she could never understand what I intended or how I was feeling, I slumped down on the hard bunk where she'd slept the past two nights. Could the child never understand that I only wanted what was best for her? Did she mean it when she insisted that even this was something which was none of my business or that I didn't understand and didn't need to worry about? Did she really mean to act like I was making mountains out of molehills? Involuntarily, I armoured myself against her. I expected to see the frosty stubbornness in her face or even that sarcastic look of contempt which she could assume when she wanted to hurt me as much as possible.

But none of this did I see. She was perfectly calm. She stood in the middle of the cell in her blue jeans and blue cotton shirt, so crumpled it was obvious she'd been sleeping in it, and her fair hair loose – they'd taken the hairclip off her – and she looked at me calmly, no . . . there was even a trace of concern in her expression as she considered me. It was just as if our roles really had been switched.

The warden had locked us in. We were alone. I wasn't allowed to be long, and I was in such a state that I was scared the time would flow through my fingers without me managing to come out with anything sensible.

We'll get you out of here, I said, like in a third-rate courtroom drama.

She smiled with encouragement. Yes, I'll be damned, she smiled at me with warmth and encouragement as if forgiving me for suddenly becoming so retarded.

Why did you do it? – I asked, discerning myself the desperation in my tone and afraid that I would turn her against me. To go and break the glass of the display case and –

I didn't break the glass, she answered.

You didn't break the glass?

No.

What do you mean? They say that –

That's what *they* say.

What are you saying? Wasn't the glass –

Yes, it did break.

It broke. Right, so you must've –

She shook her head.

I only looked through it.

The calm conviction in her answers aroused such dismay in me that my mind froze up. I was at a loss for words. I could see that she wasn't lying, at any rate not on purpose, to herself or to me, but I couldn't understand what she was saying. I stared at her. I examined her eyes closely, her face, and although I'm by no means clear about what a drug addict's supposed to look like, I saw nothing out of the ordinary. Neither could she have been kept locked up in there for so long if she was on drugs.

So was she not in her right mind? Did she really believe that her gaze alone commanded such intense magic that it could shatter glass?

Yes, of course I asked her what she'd been doing in the National Museum, in the department of antiquities of all places. In my voice: surprise, disbelief, suspicion. Teenagers these days just don't spend their time in museums, except on school trips with teachers or on organised sightseeing tours. She was clearly on no such tour. She was by herself. I've never been aware of her having any interest in antiquities. What in God's name was she doing in there surrounded by antiquities?

She turned towards me and asked calmly:

Why are you so surprised about that?

Why? What a question! Should I remind her of her pop phase, the winter she sang with Hoarse and Glandular, should I remind her of the nights when Social Services brought her home, or should I remind her of Óli? But that would have been unnecessary. Normal teenagers just don't visit museums unless they're studying something in connection with them. I could of course have said that studying didn't seem to have been foremost in her mind these past few years and that she wouldn't have gone and broken the glass if her visit had been prompted by such a change of character, but I let it lie because I didn't dare start a quarrel about the glass, and was about to nip this discussion in the bud when she asked once again:

Why aren't I allowed to show an interest in old stuff?

It's difficult to explain to you how this made me feel. It remains for you to understand it better when we get home.

Of course it was an idiotic question which, before this happened, you wouldn't have given a second thought. But all stubbornness has vanished from her. No longer does she hiss like a cornered animal defending itself. She asks as if she means to get an answer. She even seems to be interested in hearing what you've got to say. She waits.

Suddenly I see that I've locked my hands so tightly together that my knuckles are turning white, as if I expect my fingers otherwise to start wriggling about all over the place of their own accord in some sort of nervous pitter-patter. It's a child's habit, from the time when I had to own up when faced with accusations I didn't understand. Why isn't she *allowed* to show an interest in old stuff? I never said that she wasn't *allowed* . . . she speaks as if I've planted the idea in her head that there's some kind of taboo on museums. Ridiculous! Of course we could have taken her to the National Museum in Iceland, had it only occurred to us to do so. But we're just not in the habit of striding off to museums. She knows that. All the same I felt at this moment that she viewed us as conspirators who had deliberately denied her initiation into some holy mystery . . . God, how strange this suddenly all seemed to me . . . I'd become so bewildered that for a moment it seemed to me that my guilt towards her consisted solely of never having taken her to a museum when she was little. Then I grasped the fact that she wasn't accusing me. She'd given up accusing me. I couldn't get rid of my own guilt. She would no longer take it off me. My fingers relaxed and I gave her no answer. I just shook my head and she didn't press me for an answer, as if she knew that finding one would be beyond me. But that doesn't alter the fact that I'm asking myself:

Why did we never take her to a museum? Maybe because no-one took me to a museum when I was little? That I can recall. Why did no-one ever take me to a museum?

She stood by this testimony of hers, that she hadn't broken the glass. She said that she'd seen she had time to spare and had wandered – that's how she put it herself, never having admitted that anything had been arranged beforehand – she wandered, that is, into a section of the museum where prehistoric exhibits are on display. Bodies, what's more. Said that she'd been startled at first. Several thousand years old, they were there on display in glass cabinets, bodies that had been found in oak coffins inside grave-mounds, and some in bogs. The bog-people didn't decay. They were so well preserved that some still had hair on their heads and nails on their fingers. Stained a little brown from their long repose in the bogs, but more or less intact. Calmly and patiently these people were lying there, as if they'd left their physical forms behind in this museum and were planning on returning. And even the mound-dwellers who had lost their flesh could still return if they got a move on. Their skeletons lay there in their clothes, and they could put their hair and their nails back on and carry on smiling out at Dís like the woman lying over there. She was smiling so broadly that her teeth reached nearly all the way out to her ears. She had taken nothing with her into the otherworld except a beaker made from birch-bark which lay at her feet. I felt for her so badly when I saw the beaker, said Dís. Not because she was so poor, but because now everybody could see that she'd placed all her trust in the beaker. If she wanted to come back.

Her life contained in this one object. She was so vulnerable. Everybody could see how she could be harmed. She could fool nobody. Neither could the man over there with the big gold ring around his neck. He didn't even have clothes. Stark naked. Needed encouraging. Don't be afraid of slipping back into your skin, Dís said to him. With that amazing gold ring around your neck, no-one will see that you're naked.

She'd been craftier, this one in the long skirt with the robe wrapped around her, with wires of gold wound about her ears, with arm-rings of pure gold which coiled like snakes up her arms, and with her thick hair twisted with coiled bands and wound into countless rings around her head so that it rose like a mountain, no, like a crown on her head; she was so well prepared that she had the comb for her hair fastened at her girdle. But Dís hovered longest in front of the young girl in the hip-skirt. She stood in front of her for a long time as if she wanted to invoke her into saying something about herself. Was she a long-lost relative of the straw-skirted dancing girls in Honolulu? The hip-skirt, which was bordered at the top and bottom, was made from twisted strands of wool so that you could just make out the hair on her groin. Around her waist was a belt, the belt-plate beautifully adorned with eddying whirls, and about her arms and in one ear she wore rings. At her feet was yet another container made of birch-bark. There had been mead in the bark beaker, made from wheat and berries, herbs and honey . . . everything dried up in the beaker now . . . she'd hopefully find the way back to her body all the same . . . and then it was as if Dís lost herself in all these golden rings and beakers which filled whole cabinets. Over there was a statue of a goddess with both eyes made of gold, dressed in a hip-skirt; before her there coils a fantastic beast with a snake's body and the head of a horse and she's kneeling or sitting with one hand raised as if she's grasping a rein . . . in a well and in beakers and pots were sacrificial gifts to appease the goddess or to thank her: women's jewellery, braids of hair, rings and riding gear . . .

Then she saw the sun-horse. Standing on a wagon he pulled a shining, gilded disc. She'd never seen a more beautiful horse.

So delicate and sensitive in its sturdiness. The opposites were in such perfect harmony, she said, that I saw straight away that this was a spiritual horse. A celestial draught-animal. No-one was so sublimely humble unless he could sense how noble his role was. I seemed to know him. I seemed to carry him in my heart. Yes, those were her words, and in this state of mind she stopped at the gold cabinet. Pure gold. Beauty beyond description. Never seen anything like it! Gold in everything there, gold in the cups with the long snake-handles ending in horse-heads, and gold in the beaker. For there was the beaker. Decorated on the outside with a chain of whorls which coiled around the bowl like a ring, and within this formal ring each whorl coiled like a snake until it unravelled again to form the next whorl, and in this way the ending of one was the beginning of another so that nowhere in it was there beginning or ending, but everything was joined up in an endless ring like eddying water in an eternal cycle, and on the inside at the bottom of the bowl a ring was formed and within the ring, a cross. So bright was the gleam which came from this beaker that it seemed to be spurning the glass which enclosed it. I was dazzled by it, she said, and then I don't remember anything else but the mirror. It stood behind the beaker, lit up by its golden glow. It was positioned against a pillar and so tilted back slightly as if it were inviting everybody going by to look at their reflection. The handle was short and formed in three sections. Its lowest section was a ring; in the middle, an oval loop connected at the top to a bow-shaped loop which finally curved around the mirror like a frame. The mirror itself was circular. Gradually Dís could make out ornamentation through the dazzle. There was a peculiar harmony between the shape of the handle and the ornamentation on the mirror. But on the mirror the ring was open at the top like a beaker or bowl and the oval rings curled outwards from there to both sides like the orbits of eyes, and inside them were circles which stared out like pupils. The mirror was a face which was turned towards her.

Dís thought this was fun. She bowed exuberantly, wished it good day and then waited smiling as if to find out how the face would receive her greeting. Saw her reflection appear but . . . no, that wasn't her. It couldn't be. Those were different features entirely! Creepy. The ornamentation distorted the lower part of the face. The corners of the mouth stretched downwards and the smile became a horseshoe of a grimace which stretched out to the sides of the bowl and merged with its bottom. Then she saw that the mouth was open, wide open, like a scream, and inside this screaming mouth was a circle which enclosed an abyss. Frightened, she gazed into the mirror's eyes. For a moment she looked eye-to-eye with bottomless despair, then she made out a tiny glimmer of light, as if a trace of hope had been kindled in these eyes. They were holding their breath with the effort of fixing her fast, these blue eyes set deep in a face swathed in thick fair hair, which was billowing around the frame of the mirror as if she were standing on the other side of it as well, and were watching her image from there through a mask. Or was someone else?

These eyes drew Dís towards them with such power that she couldn't break away from them. She felt as if she were sinking into them . . . she was drawn always closer and downwards, until her head started to swim . . . felt as if she were falling, but then was sucked as fast as a gust of wind as if through a deep well towards the light in these eyes, until she stood opposite them, and in front of her was a young fair-haired woman who was slowly putting the mirror down without taking her eyes off her. In the blue of the eyes, quick sparkles of light glittered like an unspoken language. Expectancy and quiet amazement were in her voice when she whispered:

You've come!

As if she'd been awaited.

Dís was dumbstruck. She cast her eyes around the place to try to get her bearings. But it was so dark inside that she could see nothing to begin with. Utter darkness laid its heavy paw over everything around her. The mirror which had glittered so prettily had lost its brightness, and now reflected nothing but darkness. The sheen of the woman's golden hair had faded, and in the long dark cloak she was dressed in it would hardly

29

have been possible to make her out if it hadn't been for the eyes. They alone smouldered. No other ember was burning in there. A very slight, almost indiscernible odour of damp was in the air. No movement anywhere in this darkness: everything was static and yet swollen with expectation, as if Dís's reaction counted. Little by little her eyes got used to the darkness and she began to pick out dull outlines. She found herself in some sort of space. The walls were made from massive stones, taller than a man, and the chamber was roughly oval. The ceiling was not high but slightly vaulted. Also made from stones. She saw no windows but thought she could make out an opening in the ceiling, but a stone had been laid across it so that not a glint of daylight filtered in. Was she inside a tower or a rock? Instinctively she started to look for a doorway. How had she got here? She turned around. She caught a brief glimpse of a man's shadow, a man in a long dark coat and hood. He slipped furtively along the walls towards a low doorway as if he had been spying, but when he was just about to pass through the doorway he turned his head and looked at Dís. His left eye-socket was empty. She stared into this unseeing hole for a moment before the darkness swallowed him. A chill spread through her and instinctively she drew closer to the woman as if seeking protection. But the woman paid no heed to the shadow. She didn't take her eyes off Dís and there was a silent waiting in her look, as if she were making an appeal. When Dís sensed how forlorn she was, her fear vanished. What did this woman expect of her? You've come, she'd said.

Where am I? asked Dís.

You are Gunnlöth's guest, the woman answered.

Dís, I said cautiously. You don't have to make this up for my benefit. You can tell me the truth.

That's what happened, she said.

She'd told the lawyer the same story.

The ambassador provided this lawyer for me. He'd already spoken to Dís when I went to meet him the first time. To tell you the truth I heaped curses on the embassy when I went for the first consultation. To bring me here! I felt as if it had been done to shame me. His office was on a narrow side-street not far from Strøget. On both sides of the street there stood tall rows of connecting buildings built from dark-grey stone. Ancient. The street was grey and little-travelled even though it was only a stone's throw from all the crowds and all the shops on Strøget. Perhaps that's why it struck me as being so alien. I felt I'd suddenly and unexpectedly arrived in another city and another era. A sign in the lobby said that his office was up on the third floor. No lift. I had to trudge up worn stone steps which wound in curves between cold stone walls. Never had I imagined that I'd need to turn to a lawyer in a court case. But had I done so . . . had I ever staged myself in this role as if I were in a film, automatically I would have envisaged a bright and spacious office. Painted white. With an impeccably smart secretary and a respectable lawyer in pressed trousers. I would no doubt have taken as given a respectable crime and a respectable lawyer who always received payment. But there I was now, sitting opposite this lawyer. Papers and documents lay heaped on his desk. The windows bare, if blinds of the type that gather dust don't count. Actually, to give him his due they seemed to be clean. But the clothes on him! Without a tie. And wearing sandals! If there's one thing I can't stand, it's men in sandals. It's a short step from there to seeing their bare toes and the shirt open at the neck.

But the ambassador had told me that he was the most able lawyer in such cases. He had the most experience of assisting teenagers who'd got themselves into a scrape. He'd even helped Icelandic teenagers who'd got into a scrape. That's how he put it. I felt he was dragging me down into some . . . some mire . . . some public mire where everybody slaps everybody else down in their efforts to get up out of the filth until the mud sucks you down and you sink and become part of it like a senseless worm. I wanted to stand in my own private mud pool from where you could see dry land, and to be able at least, if nothing better came along, to wait sensibly for it to dry up without losing control of myself. Or step straight up out of it. I'll sort this out! We'll sort this out! Deep down, this is what I wanted people to see in me. Even though Dís had got herself into a tangle . . . yes, *tangle* was the right word . . . we only had to comb out the tangle . . . untangle this hitch . . . have it all orderly and straightened out. Unpick this Gordian knot. Step up out of the mud pool. My child *must not* be allowed to sink. Not mine. Not me and Dís.

I was mortified when the ambassador added that the lawyer assisted these youths free of charge. But straight away I crafted for myself a golden bridge out of money, out of the public mire and over into my private mud pool. Said:

Of course I'm paying!

The ambassador seemed taken aback. He became flustered when he tried to dig himself out of it. Stammered: yes, yes, of course, and I didn't mean . . .

How do you like that!

And so I began my talk with the lawyer by informing him that I would pay the asking price. And he answered that that would come in handy.

As if I were doing it for his benefit!

Then we started to discuss Dís's case and I resolved to be

rational and let his clothing and lack of formality pass. If he were the man most likely to be of help to Dís then . . . well, he should at least be given a go.

He said that getting her acquitted would be difficult and maybe impossible. She'd been caught red-handed. And although she hadn't got away with the beaker, this was no run-of-the-mill shoplifting offence. A price couldn't be put on it. It was one of the jewels of the museum.

I just can't conceive what she was doing in a museum.

I know full well that this was a stupid remark. Either I was losing my touch, or perhaps I was feeling my way along. Some hidden instinct told me I should assume the blank expression, this mask of innocence and vulnerability which down-trodden women are prone to putting on when they're manipulating other people in order that it should go practically unnoticed. I did this, when I'd resolved always to steer a set course. Never to drift with the wind.

The gold beaker is thought to be two to three thousand years old . . . a unique object . . . found by chance in a peat bog earlier this century . . . it's thought to have been some kind of sacred artefact used in ceremonies . . . inlaid with ancient religious symbols . . .

I said that this ghastly business was beyond me and that Dís could hardly have grasped what kind of object this was. And then young people didn't rate that kind of thing too highly nowadays . . .

He said that it would be hard to claim that she hadn't realised what kind of object this was, in a museum where all the information about the exhibits was at hand. She seemed to be a sensible girl. Even when she told this peculiar story.

He flicked through police reports. The girl in the ticket booth says she remembers her. There aren't so many visitors to the museum on weekdays, especially at this time of year, before the stream of tourists begins. And then the prehistory department isn't visited much either by locals or visitors from overseas. Dís had arrived mid-morning. Was arrested after midday. It might be added, the lawyer said as he put down the report, that there aren't many guards because of cuts in culture spending. By no means a guard in every room. They have to walk from room to room to keep watch and most of them are old and frail. There was for example no guard in the room and no other visitors when . . . and here he hesitated slightly . . . when the glass broke. She was standing with the beaker in her hands when they got to her, but didn't seem to have tried to get away.

She can't have been herself, I said. She wouldn't have known what she was doing . . . been there the whole day . . . without food . . . who knows, maybe she hadn't eaten for days on end . . .

He made no reply to this. Just looked pensively down at the table, stroking both his eyebrows. He was either reading something out of this heap of reports or he thought it not worth the trouble of answering me. At last he looked up and regarded me a little intently as if meaning to make a mental note of my reaction as he said:

The investigation will doubtless be directed at whether she was acting in collusion.

In collusion?

In collusion with some group.

And when he saw my furrowed brow he added:

Some group with an agenda.

A group with an agenda! I could barely work out what he was going on about, but I finally asked, struck with astonishment, whether he meant a terrorist group, because suddenly an angry voice sprang to mind which crept into my ear-holes and screamed: a *political terrorist*; now others as well as you seemed to have gone a little crazy, and it struck me that people abroad must have become unhinged out of a grotesque paranoia, and that such silliness belonged nowhere except in an over-the-top crime film. And when he said yes, I asked in a shocked voice just what sort of a notion that was, actually? Aside from the fact that Dís had never meddled in politics, it was hard to understand what use political terrorists thought they would have for a beaker from a museum of antiquities.

There are terrorist groups around which practise art theft. In Ireland for instance.

In Ireland, yes, but my dear fellow, Dís is Icelandic . . . Icelanders don't engage in terrorist activities.

No, he said and stood up and started to walk indifferently about the floor in his sandals as if this whole conversation had had no other purpose than to intimidate me. And added, light in tone as if we were exchanging pleasantries about the weather:

Icelanders only engage in drugs and petty theft and criminal negligence. But it's not out of the question that they're starting to turn their minds to crimes on a global scale.

I paid no attention to this Danish humour. Thought it far from appropriate as things stood. He sat back down. And said that this strange story of hers could be a clever trick to disguise some other purpose and throw the authorities off the scent. These people came up with some funny things. And I sensed that I'd rolled my eyes to heaven, a thing I do when I don't want to make a secret of how stupid I think people are being. Then he sighed out loud as if this had become some sort of war between us conducted in code and offered me coffee, as long as I could drink it black. I accepted the offer and actually I was glad. Could relax. Could feel how stiff in the back I'd become and tired in the arms, even though I'd been resting my hands in my lap the whole time. As if I'd been toiling away. I became almost meek as he plodded back and forth across the floor in sandalled feet between the electric coffee pot in the corner and the desk where, on top of letters and documents, he put two paper cups of coffee in plastic holders. He drank the coffee in a few gulps and was silent. I drank more slowly. The coffee was slightly stale like it always is from electric pots, but the warmth relaxed my tense muscles. When he had finished the cup he pushed it away from him and started to speak in an everyday, conversational tone. Asked if I could give him no clue as to the reason for all this or what could have made her do it. Whether I could tell him something about ourselves and our relationship with Dís.

You own a contracting company as a couple?

Asked this in such a way as to break the ice. And I said that my husband was an engineer and I was trained in business and that we had set up the company as young newly-weds soon after we finished college. We'd started with small means, well, empty-handed really, but we'd had the luck to get enough jobs right from the start and then Dís had been born and when Dís was little I'd actually thought we were a model family . . . proud of one another and contented with one another . . . yes, and as you say, we look after the business together . . . that's why we hadn't both been able to get away at present . . . we were continually branching out . . . and suddenly and almost without realising it I've got into this state where I'm like two people . . . it's a silent split because I'm practised in it . . . out loud I rattle on about our unfathomable difficulties with Dís of late and I've got the spiel off by heart, but my mind has rushed off home, wrapped up in the drawings on the desk . . . the offer of a job on Reykjanes . . . my thoughts are glued to them as the import of everything the lawyer's been saying about a terrorist group comes home with full force: if our child is suspected of a terrorist act, we won't get the job. Even though the job isn't military in nature, it's still connected with the Airbase and two governments will need to approve, maybe military authorities, and it could all be misconstrued, and while I reel off that rather than prepare for exams she was idling her time away composing poetry – but it's being offered by Icelanders – and then she'd sung in a band – but we'll still need to be above suspicion ... and it's at this point that I reflect on whether or not we'd grasped this . . . was this the reason you said it . . . was this the reason I emphasised mental illness rather than a completely sober crime? No, I'm not that unscrupulous . . . it can't be . . . it didn't even occur to me . . . I was only thinking about . . . I wanted to protect her from prison, and while I said that to my knowledge her thoughts had revolved around nothing lately but this one lad, Óli, you'd have to be aware of it if your own children were wrapped up in some secret criminal alliance . . . not my Dís, always so forthright; then an absolutely appalling shiver of disgust went through me as I perceived us being drawn into a context which was such a far cry from our own world view. People who were just trying to make it through. Securing their future, and that anyone – our own child among them – should judge us on an international scale as if we were criminals . . . no, unthinkable! For my logic has reached a dead-end. No-one has said that the theft of the beaker was meant to injure us. I've got to put a stop to this grotesque way of thinking right now. *This is too absurd by far.* Finally I quietened down on both fronts. And the lawyer, light in tone as if I'd been reeling off a funny story for him, said:

Well! We'll see. It's possible that she intended to steal the beaker for herself, though it's implausible. To decorate her window-sill. Or to use it to serve her friends cheap white wine from Bulgaria. She couldn't have sold it. She must have realised that.

You can't be so sure. Dís isn't very orderly in her way of thinking, I said, but all authority had gone from my voice.

It makes matters even worse that she should make this story up. If she's showing the court disrespect or off-handedness. The act itself, to intend to steal from the museum in broad daylight, is bad enough in its own right. This is out of the ordinary.

I believe, I said, that both the act and the story show that something must have come over her. That has to be it. I know that she's not . . . never has been . . . seriously into theft. Neither does she have terrorist connections. I just don't believe it. Something must have happened to her. Something which has unbalanced her. She would have told me the truth if she'd been planning on stealing the beaker. Dís isn't devious. She's not a liar and she doesn't do that sort of thing – not in an ill-meaning way; sometimes I've even felt that she could have avoided various, shall we say, confrontations if she hadn't been so stubborn. It could be more peaceful . . . at home I mean, if she weren't always so sure of her opinions . . . I mean . . . but still . . . well, you probably know teenagers . . . all sorts of things can possess them . . . but then they get over it, of course . . . Dís will get over it . . .

I didn't know whether he had listened to me through to the end. But I didn't miss the thoughtfulness in his expression when he contemplated me and said after a moment's silence:

Well, if nothing new comes out in the near future it's just as likely that the Crown Prosecutor will ask for a psychiatric assessment himself. Then again, it might be clever if I got in there first.

Yes, I said.

We'll have to weigh it up.

Now he became brusque once more, and I was maybe too eager so I thought it better to say nothing more for the time being. For a moment he looked down at the surface of his desk without speaking and his fingers played almost of their own accord on the table. Then he looked up and his gaze was searching. Now I got the feeling that I was being examined or interrogated.

Who was this Gunnlöth?

Who?

This question came as a surprise to me, though you might not believe it. I laughed uneasily. I wasn't prepared for it. Hadn't in the least been expecting the conversation to take this turn.

That's just some nonsense ... it could just as well have been ...

Who was she? – he asked again, a little sharply, and again I was reminded of how quick this man seemed to be in changing his manner. Now I pictured him as a grave detective in the movies who's caught scent of a clue which could expose an entire crime ring.

She's in the *Edda*, I said; Odin stole the art of poetic invention from her.

Then I couldn't remember anything else.

And how the hell could I possibly be expected to remember anything else? I don't care what they say on red-letter days about Icelanders' love of literature. You don't go poring over the *Edda* on a day-to-day basis. To be honest with you, it was very unlike me to remember anything from the *Edda* at all.

I stood up quickly. I'd started to feel bad. As if I had something to answer for.

He said that he could apply for permission for me to visit Dís more often than twice a week seeing as we were foreigners.

I thanked him. Said I accepted the offer. Very grateful. Said I was on my way to her now. Said I was confident that the truth would come out. Tried to be brisk, with a bit of bravado, tried to arouse his confidence in me. Spoke like a scout leader. And he responded in kind. Said that it would be something new if the truth came out in a courtroom. We ought at the very most to hope for justice.

Then he looked amicably at me as he'd done when he gave me the coffee and an anxious expression came over him which I would have called fatherly if Dís had been his daughter. I don't believe in the usefulness of shutting teenagers up in prisons. If you could only get to the bottom of why she's telling this story . . .

I suddenly became flustered in the face of his sincerity. Shook his hand good-bye. Couldn't find my gloves. They weren't to be found either in my handbag or anywhere in the mess of documents on the table. It looked like I'd left them at the hotel. I'd come here with no gloves on without realising it. My naked hands hung down from my sleeves like foreign bodies when I left. I had to walk a short distance before I could find a taxi. Felt worse and worse the nearer I got to the crowds. Looked no-one in the face. Stopped at no shop window. Not because I was late, but because I felt I needed to hide. As if I feared I would be found out in the open air among other people. Hurried into the taxi as if I were on the run, and whispered to him where I was going. To the prison.

I tried to convince myself that it was perfectly natural that I should be preoccupied over having a daughter in prison. But knew that that wasn't the sole reason for the state I was in. Within me the knowledge stirred that I was not just on my way to the prison. I was going on a quest which had been forced upon me. And I couldn't account for why this quest caused me such anxiety. It was like having a bad taste in your mouth long after a meal without knowing what had disagreed with you so badly. Try and find out what's going on with this story, he'd said.

Gunnlöth! Who was she? Does anybody know?

Odin stole the art of poetic invention from her, I'd said. Then I couldn't remember anything else. It was true. I knew nothing . . . remembered nothing. Apart from this. And the nearer we got to the prison the heavier the question weighed on my mind: how come I thought I remembered this?

But said to myself – while I paid the taxi driver and explained who I was to the guard at the prison gate and walked through the yard and then along the corridor behind the warden in to Dís – that obviously she wouldn't keep this story up. I didn't believe she would. I didn't believe her wits were actually impaired. An act of terrorism? No! Maybe something had come over her. Yes. But nothing serious. Not crazy. And so what if she *were* lying to escape punishment? I wasn't going to blow her cover! She just hadn't yet realised that I meant to shield her at all costs . . . that she could trust me. She didn't need to string me along.

Why have I come here? – I asked and looked at Gunnlöth, perplexed.

Dís! Dís dear, you don't need to keep this up. Not for my benefit. Don't do this.

Come with me, said Gunnlöth and held out her hand to me as if to lead me further into this shadowy world.

You have to trust me. Don't you understand that I'm trying to get you free?

I took her hand without hesitating.

Half-heartedly I decided to wait. To allow her to continue. She would have to give this up at some point. No two ways about it. In spite of this odd, distant look which caused me more anxiety than I dared to admit to myself just now, I tried to convince myself that she was just acting . . . making up some fantasy . . . she was bound to stop this. She was bound to spare me this. But until then I had no other choice but to go along with her. And so I asked:

Why? Why did you take her hand?

Curiosity, said Dís. Said that she'd got really excited, like in the treasure hunt when she was little. You remember that game? The treasure was hidden but could be found by means of clues in the form of riddles and symbols which had to be solved, and the solution led you on to yet more hidden places . . . a fresh riddle . . . onwards, further; and hot on the scent she ran off to search . . . the outstretched arm was like the ball of twine which magically shows the way in the fairy tales. She meant to follow it.

Curiosity! The same answer she gave me whenever I asked her why she was out whole nights at a time. Curiosity. Gathering experience. But God help me! There *is* a difference between running around with common-or-garden idiots who switch day for night and letting yourself be drawn into the abyss of insanity.

But you must have realised . . . Weren't you scared?

Yes, she said dead calmly. She knew somehow that there would be no turning back if she took hold of this outstretched hand. It seemed as if she would be taking an obligation upon herself; she didn't know what it involved but suspected it was connected with this darkness. Wasn't sure whether she wanted to know anything about it.

Yes, but . . .

I'd become impatient, fervent, as if I were talking her out of something which it was in my power to prevent. I didn't want her to go. Where would Gunnlöth take her? She would have to endure horror and suffering if she went on this journey. I

41

couldn't bear that thought. I wanted to protect her, shelter her from the wickedness of the world, hold her in a magic circle so that no harm should come to her. In my fervour I forgot that it wasn't possible to prevent any of it. She'd come back, no . . . she was still on this journey and now, by means of her narrative, she was going to drag me along with her right from the beginning. Yes, that's what was filling me with fear. I had to follow her. And whether this journey was truth or lie or invention, I was almost giving in to the fear of the suffering in store for me . . . I wanted to run away . . . why couldn't she spare me this?

Why did you go then? Seeing that you were afraid?

An oddly tender smile passed over her face. She regarded me silently a moment, and I realised that I was swaying back and forth like an anxious old woman who has nothing else to resort to. I tried to steel myself but I waited on tenterhooks for the answer as if I had everything staked on it. Dís put her hands round both of mine and in her firm young grip my hands too seemed old and anxious.

I felt for Gunnlöth so much. Her hand was speaking out of such an exposed loneliness that I had no other choice. Gunnlöth was asking me for something that she couldn't say out loud. She was begging me to understand something or to do something which she couldn't put into words. And this was so important . . . like an appeal which had laid claim to her spirit, and when I listened I heard anguish as if she had endured inexpressible suffering. Or had it still in store. Gunnlöth's suffering gave me strength.

It got a bit brighter as I held my hand out to Gunnlöth. Not much. But enough that I saw to my astonishment that there was a dark-clad creature hidden behind Gunnlöth. This world seemed full of shadows. But this one stood still, so deadly still that at first sight she seemed carved out of stone. A statue of a woman. She wore a wide black robe which hid her completely and a hood which was pulled forwards over her brow. And although she stood so still and not a fold of cloth stirred, her posture betrayed no stillness, no peace. It was as if the air around her was throbbing. She was small and stooped and stretched her chin forwards to follow what we were doing. She was so full of fervour that she seemed about to burst out of the stone. To try and come to life. Make the stone speak. She didn't open her mouth, but the face, which was more ancient than any face I've ever seen before, was scored by deep wrinkles which looked like letters. The lines criss-crossed. As if the sculptor had carved words there which you should have been able to read, if he hadn't continually written new words on top of the old ones. As if everything he knew – or she knew … as if a place needed to be found for the whole world's knowledge in this single face.

I couldn't take my eyes off her. And I wondered whether Gunnlöth was aware of her. Or was she going to ignore her like she did the furtive shadowy creature in the hat?

But Gunnlöth was aware of her. She looked at her and there was such a strange expression on Gunnlöth's face where love and tenderness and inquisitiveness played, and even uncertainty tinged with fear. Then she nodded, unnoticeably almost. As if she could read something in the face.

And the eyes of this stone-struck hood-woman came to life. They were like a vixen's as they shot from one to the other of us. Then she stared at me so fixedly that the hood trembled. No doubt about it. She was sending me some message so strong that it was as if I'd become paralysed, and embers were smouldering in her eyes which would turn into tongues of flame in a second if I didn't do as she wanted. It was from her that the will flowed. Locked in stone but alive. I shuddered at the terrible power of this will should it burst out of the stone. And she was so clever with spells that I felt she was sending *me* this will, making *me* will something. *I* was supposed to will something. And Gunnlöth held my hand tight and started to pull on it. They wanted to show me something.

After that I had no choice. Even if I'd tried to turn back, this stone-struck hood-woman would have bent my will in this one direction . . . onwards, without me being able to do a thing about it.

I awaited what was to come like a person condemned to

death.

Where was I being taken?

It was late in the afternoon when the visit was over and I walked out of the prison. Not many people about in the street. I couldn't see a taxi anywhere, and I didn't know how the buses ran. I hadn't been up to organising a cab for myself and the state I was in robbed me of all my initiative. I wasn't in the mood to go back inside to phone, and I set off in what I thought must be the direction of the city centre. I knew my way around Copenhagen, though never before had I had call to pick out winding paths between psychiatrists and the police. God almighty! And the whole time you were tucked up at home, in the jacuzzi downstairs perhaps, or sailing along the streets of the neighbourhood, the Mercedes as your flag ship … no, you were slaving away at the office or in a meeting, of course. I was just feeling so bad. The last light of day was quickly disappearing. With so few people and in the sinking twilight, the street seemed to take on an otherworldly look, as if at the turning point of day and night, that moment when everything hangs in an uncertain balance an instant before all thoughts sink towards night, and everything was enlivened as if to forebode a night when nothing would lie still. The cars streaming past were going at such breakneck speed that they reminded me of racehorses, all stretching their bodies forwards in the same direction; one of them braked suddenly beside me and a megaphone shot out of the window: Don't forget the meeting … then it was gone, and just then a dog started barking and howling at me from behind head high iron railings alongside the pavement, and I felt as if all the monsters of the night would break free of their fetters and drag me off with them. Dís, and this bad taste in my mouth ... were we going out of our minds?

I didn't know which way I should head, being in no rush to get back to the hotel for dinner. I couldn't imagine taking my seat in the brightly-lit dining room where everything glinted as if you were under a spotlight. I couldn't imagine being under a spotlight! Could it be that I felt I belonged among those forces which were only waiting to break free and take over?

Ahead of me I saw the sign of somewhere to eat. I picked up my pace. As luck would have it, this wasn't a bright neon sign which, glinting and giggling neurotically, tries to announce its presence and draw as big a crowd as possible. I wasn't seeking the light, like I've already told you. I don't know why not. We just didn't have much to do with each other right now, me and the light. The sign was made of glass and filthy dirty, and the curtains hung a grubby greyish white and limp with wear and tear in the window; certainly wouldn't have survived one more wash, a wash that could prove costly to the owner and had been put off for that reason. Through the window-pane I saw that the table cloths inside were red-checked. That's sensible if you need to save on laundry – or on fabric. Suddenly the door opened and three teenagers came bursting out, laughing and chattering and boisterous, and I shrunk back, felt I had to get away and instinctively started casting my eyes about me for a place to hide, some bolthole, but the kids were off at once on growling motor-bikes, and I could no longer ignore what the beating of my heart was telling me: I'm scared of teenagers. I feel threatened by them.

I know that teenagers have been known to attack people, of course. It's only rational to be on your guard. But my reason also tells me that not all teenagers attack people. I'm not afraid of an assault. No instinct to put up a fight was triggered in me. Only fear ... and flight. I'm scared of teenagers. You never know what's going on in their heads. There's no telling what horrors to expect from them. Even teenagers who sit well-groomed and well-behaved on living-room sofas with their mums and dads as guards beside them – if there are teenagers like that still around – cause me anxiety. They'll manage to pull some stunt quite unaccountably and out of the blue, every bit as much as a teenage girl in a half-empty museum, and there outside this grimy eating place I realised that deep down I've always known of this fear and now in the ominous atmosphere of the street it sprouted shoots as if finally having received the right kind of nourishment.

When I walked inside I realised that I was hungry. I could have stuffed myself. It was as if this revolting greasy fug of garlic and beer which clung to everything in the place whet my appetite. I crept like a sleepwalker to an empty table in the corner, sat down and waited, and it wasn't until I heard a woman's husky voice announcing over everybody else, in a not unfriendly way, but with an ironic silkiness: Perhaps madam is waiting for the maitre d', and everybody started laughing, that I realised that you obviously had to serve yourself here. I stood up and walked over to the counter. Everybody's eyes were on me of course, and to my fright I found that I was forcing the corners of my mouth into the creases of a smile as if to show that I had a sense of humour, even when the humour was aimed at me in the form of a derisive ticking-off. Just like a beggar, in spite of the ten-thousand-crown suit and the Bally shoes from Switzerland. And then the faces at the tables altered their expression. They smiled amicably at me, with encouragement even; one flabby old man even shook his head in a resigned way, as if to say that there was indeed a lot that had to be put up with. It was as if they'd taken me into some sort of society. A shudder ran through me, because poverty and hard luck hung over these people, and not only that but some sort of timelessness. Nowhere was there any trace of shame or sadness, as if they had no recollection of anything better … as if they'd known all along that they'd probably wind up there … yes, like they'd been sitting there since time immemorial and would continue to sit there, this bloated flabby old man in braces and crumpled shirt open at the neck, and a woman with red curves drawn far out past her lips like a clown and when she opened her mouth to swig from her beer mug the lines reached out to her cheeks, and the little old woman with the head-scarf hunched over her beer mug darting her eyes sideways at me so sharply that she didn't seem able to move them back into place, and the husky voice asked me what I wanted. I said I wanted sausages because nothing else came to mind, and she said it'd take a couple of minutes, and did I want to wait or—? … and the question in the wave of her hand and in her eyes – where, deep beneath the friendliness, however, there were still traces of an ironic glint – showed that she was giving me a route out of here, offering me a chance, but I looked her straight in the eye and said I'd wait. Then without further ado she stuck a large pair of tongs into a pot of sausages and fished out two sausages which had been simmering away there in tepid water for so long that the fat had hardened into a white crust on them, and slapped them onto a plate with chips, asking: Beer? – and when I made no reply she slammed a mug of beer down in front of me. And carrying this, I went back to the table.

And then I sat there with sausages and a mug of beer in front of me, and though I still felt the grievous hunger which had come over me, I didn't start right away because I was cowing my stomach into submission. Food and drink. This is food and drink, I said to my stomach: eat, drink – you don't deserve anything better … why the hell I was thinking like this, all the while staring at a burnt-out candle in the middle of the table, hardly visible for the hardened wax which had trickled down and piled up, like lifeless lava from a prehistoric eruption whose original fire is death itself … and with this in front of me I started to eat and drink and I was gripped by the bizarre feeling that I was cramming down the left-overs of a sacrament which had been tossed outside for the excommunicated.

The flabby man didn't take his eyes off me while I was eating. In his moist, glistening eyes there was a forthright interest … they didn't mince matters around here … still, not a nosy look, not impolite … well, yes, actually, although the look was calm and restrained, it's still rude to watch like that, or obtrusive at least, because he's watching me as if I've got nothing to hide … you have to give a person chance to hide … not gaze so mercilessly at them that they start to want to confess their sin … my sin? God almighty, why am I thinking this way? I … no … that wasn't my god … what am I thinking? What *is* the matter with me? … I'm not quite that far gone … what am I doing here? I shoved the meal away from me in disgust and stood up and the husky voice told me where I could catch a bus.

You phoned as I was on my way into the hotel room. I didn't stop to hang my coat up, throwing it on the bed as I snatched up the receiver. The bedspread had been taken off and a corner of the sheet folded over like they do in hotels. It's supposed to look like the bed is reaching out to wrap you in its arms. My bottles of nail-varnish had been lined up neatly on the dressing table. Had I turned on the light, I would no doubt have been assured that there wasn't a speck of dust or piece of rubbish that I'd left behind. But I didn't turn on the light. I sat and talked in the dark and said I'd been eating dinner late. Suddenly, the tidiness of the hotel room began to get on my nerves. I don't know why. It felt like a derisive surface to all this strange churning in my mind, just as derisive as this smooth and enticing bedspread which I knew would turn into one big tangle as soon as I started tossing and turning underneath it. I had the taste of sausages and beer in my mouth. I was convinced that the smell would carry all the way back to Iceland along the phone-line. I was trying constantly to swallow it back, this smell, this bad taste actually. I couldn't engage with anything. Your voice included. And when the voice asked what the lawyer had said, I answered: Nothing in particular. I must have played down this talk of terrorism because I don't remember us having gone on at any length about it. Our anxiety maybe just hidden on our breath, inaudible.

I don't remember when the conversation ended or what

else I said. I would no doubt have spoken with the clear voice of a recorded message. Would have given clear and adequate information. That's how it must have been. At least, I don't remember anything different. But I do remember what I kept quiet about.

Keeping quiet about my foolhardy venture into that grubby little bar is one thing. But I also kept quiet about Gunnlöth's tale.

I sat for a long time in the dark after I'd hung up and tried to work out why I'd reacted as I had. Why was I seized by this powerful feeling that I needed to hush the story up? As if I couldn't bring myself to tell you about it. Was ashamed, even. Had I been talking to a stranger, I could have persuaded myself that my silence stemmed purely from the fact that the person in question would naturally think Dís insane, and that I'd kept quiet about Gunnlöth because deep within me stirred the thought that insanity was a crime, or betrayed a shameful way of thinking. It was some kind of flaw in your personality, losing grip of day-to-day normality, morally indefensible. You don't let people know about that sort of thing.

But I wasn't talking to a stranger. And yet I got exactly the same evasive impulse as I got in the lawyer's office when he asked about Gunnlöth. And I don't understand why. As if it weren't enough to be worried about the theft of the beaker, without this on top of it all. This thing which I couldn't put my finger on. Something which mustn't get out. About whom? About Dís? So was this tale worse than the theft, then? I felt like she should have picked a different story. Why the hell couldn't she pick a different story? But there was clearly no point in losing my temper over it. This was the story that had been dealt. This story which I'd kept quiet about. And by how I'd reacted I'd drawn Dís into a conspiracy of silence. As if we were in it together. In what, though, for Christ's sake? Everything spun before me. I reached over to the bedside lamp and turned it on. Thought I'd feel better or get a hold of myself, but far from it. I flinched at this dim glow like someone found guilty of a crime. My silence belonged in the dark.

I was afraid. I wanted to go home. I'd started to feel sick. There was a bad taste in my mouth which had nothing to do with sausages and beer. I went next door and threw up in the toilet bowl. The sick floated in a horrible fatty, greeny-yellow slick on the surface of the water, tiny chunks of sausage on top like mountains in a landscape.

I sank down onto the toilet floor. My whole body was drained. Didn't have the strength to put up a fight with myself. I sat huddled up for a long time on the cold floor tiles with a wet towel pressed to my mouth. Odin stole, right ... but why this guilty feeling connected with Gunnlöth? ... this bad taste in my mouth? The person who's stolen *from* isn't the guilty one ... are they? I started to feel cold and hungry, but I didn't get up. And gradually my thoughts began to clear, like those of an ascetic who purifies his mind by fasting and punishing his own body, and it started to dawn on me that there was something dubious about this memory of mine. I went on remembering further back.

I knew then that I'd continue to keep quiet about it. Not because I thought the phone line between Iceland and Denmark wasn't up to the job, but because I found myself in a third country: in a land of guilt with my daughter Dís. That's a place you can't dial up directly.

And I had no choice but to follow along behind her ...

When I got up and looked at my reflection in the bathroom I saw the anxiety in my eyes ... the anxiety which was like a premonition of something menacing which came across in Dís's voice on my next visit to the prison, when she said:

Gunnlöth led me onwards.

At this, Hoodwoman came fully to life. She followed us. Though I never looked round, I sensed her presence always behind me. Gunnlöth led me over to the opening which the fleeing shadow had disappeared through. This doorway was so low that there was no way I could walk upright through it. Then there was a tunnel, even lower, and now I had to walk bent double. It was pitch dark in the tunnel, and the sharp odour of earth came to my nose. There was earth everywhere. Earth and stones and darkness. I was in the bowels of the earth, and though Gunnlöth took care never to walk far ahead of me, I was suddenly filled with terror … a torment I couldn't cope with, the walls of the tunnel were growing closer, they were closing in towards me, I felt they were going to collapse on me and bury me alive … I stuck my arms out to the sides to keep myself clear of the walls … there were crevices in them housing slick, wet growths, things were growing there in the dark and lizards shot down the earth walls and went between my feet, I was suffocating, my mouth opened of its own accord … I gaped greedily for air but was filled up with darkness … I couldn't cry out … now I wanted to turn back, but Hoodwoman spirited me onwards … further … onwards … until I came to a narrow opening and was flung out through it curled up in a ball … lay on the ground and started to cry … felt Gunnlöth's warm, comforting hand on my head. When I looked up I saw that the sweat was pouring off her as well.

53

Dís got to her feet.

She found herself in autumn. In an arid autumn which had taken hold in a forest clearing right at the tunnel's mouth. In the midst of the clearing, a massive tree rose up out of the parched earth. Its half-naked branches stretched over the whole clearing and disappeared into the bare, crooked branches of the forest beyond, and meshed so intricately with them that it looked more than anything like a sparse dome spreading out over infinity. This massive tree wasn't bare, but the foliage which still clung to it was mottled and withered as if no longer receiving vital sap from the stout trunk, its bark was dry and cracked, old wounds scabbed over. Beside the tree's roots was a hollow with broad, sloping sides covered in dry grey mud, and in the middle of the hollow was a black, rotten tree-trunk, hollowed out like the lining for a ruined well, the source dried up for the most part and no longer active, for the water right in the bottom of this well was stagnant, its smell like that of old ditch-water. At some point, water from this spring had flowed across the land, but now the channel was dry and arid, so grey and aimless that its meanderings petered out into the parched earth down the hillside – or mountain maybe? – because Dís couldn't see how far down to level ground it was, could only make out that she was standing on high ground. Further down the slope to the right were mounds in the landscape and for a moment she seemed to catch sight of a green sheen to one of the mounds as if there were green grass there, but it appeared only briefly and was gone like a trick of the eye into a grey mist which hung like a dead cloud over the withered vegetation. Looking over it, the country was a scorched wasteland which most resembled a landscape from the cinema in the aftermath of nuclear war. And although this was autumn, the sun could be made out through the sparse roof of the tree high up in the sky, as if it were no longer able to follow its course and didn't know where it belonged. The light it gave was dim like a dull-sighted eye, its face so introverted that it seemed to be nothing more than the stale memory of the sun of summers past, in the same way that the whole surrounding area was a vague memory of life. It was as if the vegetation had been robbed of its vitality and was no longer able to renew itself. There hung over everything an air of decline and imminent death. This sight awoke a strange sadness in Dís. The whole landscape reminded her of a woman who has been robbed of her happiness, and instantly she began to suspect something. She looked at Gunnlöth. The landscape was like Gunnlöth. Gunnlöth was ingrained in this place's silence. She stood with her head down as if scared of this landscape. And without speaking. Somewhere inside her, in a dry chest, were heavy autumn leaves.

Dís looked around for Hoodwoman. Hadn't seen her since she came out of the tunnel. But seemed to be aware of her. Sensed her presence close by. Hoodwoman creeps like a cat. She's always turned up everywhere without you noticing. Now she stood at the edge of the well, but shot a sidelong look at me, fiery-eyed. And then I'd had enough of their mysterious apathy. Could these people not explain themselves? Couldn't they say what was on their mind or did I need to drag it all out of them? I couldn't hide my impatience when I asked:

What's the matter, exactly? Why's it like this?

Hoodwoman started, and answered quickly:

Do you want to go on?

She'd hardly spoken when Gunnlöth sank down to the ground, clasped her head in her hands and rocked back and forth as if in dire distress as she began to wail – so softly at first that it was like the whispering of a gentle breeze, then ever louder and more wretchedly until the source of this measured wail no longer seemed to be inside her chest and body but in the movements of the air. The winds became restless and raged over their heads from all four cardinal directions. A groaning came from the aged tree. The whirling wind spun its gusts around the tree's crackling leaves, and the leaves' rustling became an incessant keening sucked into the spinning air. The maelstrom had become a gloomy avenue of trees clad in death sighs the colour of autumn. Gunnlöth's grief resided not only in a woman's breast, but in all creation.

I see Gunnlöth being sucked into this swirling avenue ... she's passing out of sight ... no, it's not Gunnlöth ... it's me ... I'm the one who's passing out of sight. I'm in two places at once. Abandoned by myself. I mustn't lose sight of myself ... mustn't lose myself, I had to catch up with myself before I disappeared into this dry dead avenue ... I can't move forwards ... the ground opens under my feet. I fall downwards ...

... and when I got up, the mild glow of a sinking sun was on the glade. I was alone, performing my duty before night fell. The holiest shrine of my nation was here. At the top of the hill in the middle of this holy place grows the ash tree which connects heaven and earth, and its branches spread out over all the world. Three are the roots which support it, and Urthur has told me that one is among the gods, another where the Beguiling Gulf once was, and the third over Niflheimur. Beneath the tree is the well. Of all wells, this is the holiest. Its water feeds the ash tree. Should the well dry up, heaven and earth will perish. It was my sacred duty as a priestess to sprinkle the tree with vital water from the well. I did this every evening at the point where day becomes night to ensure life's onward course. So that moon should rise, and sun. In times past, Urthur had told me, water was scooped over the entire tree so that its limbs would not lose their suppleness or decay. Now we sprinkled its trunk.

I knelt beside the well, scooped the clear pure water up in

the palms of my hands and carried it as in a beaker over to the tree. When water moistens the ash like dew the whole world of gods and men receives sustenance, and when I lay my palms to the moistened trunk and let my skin listen, I can feel my fusion with all creation.

Though late in autumn, the evening was so mild that I sat down and waited for the moon to come up so that everything could renew itself and life and death follow their natural cycle, ebb and flood alternate, rain moisten the earth and sun warm the vegetation. The ring I wore about my neck was a symbol of this cycle, and now I touched it to show my devotion to the goddess who governed all of this. I'd once happened to take this renewal for granted. I'd so often watched the waxing moon without remembering that all of this could come to an end. Urthur had told me that such an attitude was not a sign of unbounded confidence in the goddess, as I'd naively believed. I would have to take part myself, lending energy towards this renewal. I was a priestess and keeper of the holy mead …

There were no clouds, and few things gave me greater peace than seeing a waxing moon in the sky. The next full moon would be the last this year. From here I could see clearly in all directions. My vision was used to the twilight, and those places where evening shadows or woods blocked my view were filled in with images from my mind. I'd sat here so often in the eight years which had gone by since I started my training as a priestess. I'd started to see to the daily rites on my own, though Urthur still watched over me. But now my training was at an end. The ninth year was about to begin with the first moon of winter. Yes, that's why I was sitting here. The first night of the coming new year was preying on my mind. Then I was to perform for the first time the highest office of priestess. Carry the beaker in my hands. Bestow the precious mead upon the king-to-be. Entwine him in my arms. Hallow him to realm and rule.

After the new year's first night I would be a different person.

From this place I got strength. Here peace was breathed from all four cardinal directions. The trees by my father's halls down on the bank of the river stood old and dependable and wise like watchmen from the dawn of time, and the bends in the river ran calm on an evening like this. In the village down on the low ground across the river, the same tranquillity reigned. The sounds I seemed to hear were only the refrain to this evening peace. The soothing, measured flow of milk from cows' udders beneath the soft hands of the women. The sheep's ceaseless, cyclical chewing of the cud … the crackle of the home fire on the floor hearth …

I'll know when this moon is full that it's time to pick the meadwort.

I got up and walked over to the altar … the moon had risen … it threw a silvery brightness over the altar and the stones of the ring of judgement … only a few nights until full moon … and then … the mysteries … I knew about the burial ground to the north although it was hidden from the eyes of the uninitiated … Niflheimur … if he survived death he would come to me … and to the mead of life in the beaker …

At the altar I touched the ring about my neck. The ring is the rule by which my destiny is bound. I am devoted to the goddess, now and forever.

By the growing light of the moon I headed home to my lodge along the path between the trees. Everything was still. Our watchman sat on the crest of a mound outside the palisade and lulled the livestock with sleepy notes from his harp. The breeze carried the notes over this holy place. The refrain caressed the colourful autumn leaves, murmured a while by the quiet hive of the bees, resting after a busy summer, and gently brushed against the dreams of the insects who were sleeping deep underground. Even the guard at the gate was nodding off beside his sleeping hound. He knows that the surest keeper of this shrine is its very holiness. The whole world knows that no unholy person is allowed to come to us, because the goddess has her dwelling among the women here. In my chest the breath turned to song when I felt the sanctity and tranquillity of this place. That's how it's been here since ages beyond reckoning, and that's how it will be while faith in the goddess lives on in me.

When I drew near the place where we lived I caught scent of freshly-baked bread and I felt a pleasant hunger. The girls were back. All of them except Jódís. I could hear that she was in the grove behind the houses, feeding the mare. The silver-dappled moon-mare which is fairest and most holy of all beasts; no-one was to ride that mare except Jódís. I couldn't see into the grove but when she spoke to the mare Jódís's voice reached me, laden with twilight.

Suddenly, the mare's whinnying split the air. All other sounds fell silent. Just as if the whinnying burst out of the beast's throat, quick and shrill and involuntary. It took ages to die away. The air was still rippling from the echo when I walked past Urthur's weaving shed and the beat of the loom cut through it like a boat through rippling water. I was surprised to find her weaving so long after dark.

I longed to go in to ask her about the rhythm of all the worlds but didn't want to risk disturbing her. The loom's beating was firm. She says that I'm sometimes impatient. And so when I got home I went straight over to the altar at my lodge's gable end. The altar is the trunk of a felled tree with roots deep under ground. The goddess takes many forms. On the wall over the altar her highest symbol is formed in gold, the fiery wheel which encompasses the seasons, and upon the altar stands the serpent-horse. I stood by these images of the goddess, resting my eyes and my mind. Then Urthur appeared in the doorway. She looked at me. Not in the way she looks at me when I'm Gunnlöth. She looked at me as she does when I'm priestess and spoke these strange words:

Don't forget that you're a priestess.

Urthur, I whispered, reaching out both of my hands. Grasped at thin air. She was gone. She's left me alone. What makes you do this, Urthur? What makes you say that and then just leave?

There was a jangle of prison keys and the heavy door was pushed open. I all but assaulted the prison warden. I grabbed hold of his jacket collar and pleaded with him to be allowed to stay longer. I had to find out … I couldn't leave her now …

couldn't lose sight of her ... There was no expression to be seen on his face. I might have known that he'd show no mercy. In desperation, I looked at Dís. But she didn't seem to have noticed my little outburst. She felt no compassion for me. She gazed past me with regret and a forlorn love in her eyes which cut me to the marrow, because she was gazing after a different woman. For my part, I floated out of the prison cell like a shadow.

When the dog began to bark and growl at me on the other side of the fence, I realised which way I was going. The pub's sign was ahead of me. I was so distracted when I came out of the prison that I paid no attention to where I was going. I certainly didn't mean to be heading in this direction. I was exhausted. Lonely. Scared. A rattling sound came from the hound's throat as it tried to shove its muzzle through the iron bars to snap at me. I felt scared but tried to keep myself under control. Of course, I knew that the dog was locked in and wouldn't be able to get out through the fence, but fear gets over all boundaries. It can break out and trample every check and restraint underfoot until the orderly streets of reason are laid waste. The pub was not far off. I set my mind on getting there before the panic got such a hold of me that I began to run. Every nerve in my body was stretched taut in this struggle with the dog's noisy, ferocious snarling as I tried to behave as if I were oblivious to it. And suddenly, it quietened down. Finally it stopped and began to sniff. It was as if it recognised me. Sure enough, it kept up with me where I walked on the pavement on the other side of the railings, barking every now and then a little bad-temperedly as if to keep up appearances. But I'd got away without running. Even so, I carried on towards the pub.

I was overcome by a strange relief to have arrived there. As if running the gauntlet of the dog had brought me closer to the place. Or perhaps it was just the normal feeling you have towards somewhere you've been before. You know what to expect. It doesn't entirely matter how you feel about the place. What really counts is that you know what's in store for you. And I could always turn back. I hadn't actually been planning on coming back here. If it hadn't been for … if Dís hadn't carried on like that … if I'd only been allowed to find out … my hand was already on the door-handle when I suddenly pulled the silk scarf from my neck … I don't know why, because it's so ugly to have your neck uncovered … with this suit on, I mean … you're so … so under-dressed … scruffy … so … so *naked*. The rings I took off were a different matter. It's just not right, lifting a beer-glass to your lips with a ring-adorned hand.

She recognised me at once. Smiled at me and asked in her husky voice if I wanted beer. Then I sat down at the same table as before with my glass of beer. I couldn't help but notice the woman with the mouth painted out onto her cheeks, and she smiled at me as well. It surprised me that the teeth in this big, painted mouth didn't reach all the way out to her ears. I nodded slightly to her, but then hunched down over my glass. The stains on the table cloth were the same as the last time I sat here. This time they awoke in me a sense of security. I think it must have come as a shock to me that the same people as last time should be sitting there. I wasn't bold enough to examine them more closely. Needless to say it did cheer me up to some extent that the women should remember me, but at the same time I found it jarring that they didn't seem surprised I'd come. As if they'd known all along that I'd be heading back there. This was going too far. I hadn't come in order to strike up an acquaintance with anybody here, I was after all a customer of an altogether different ilk … events had just conspired in this way … if Dís … What was I to do? Why was I sitting here swilling down beer among … among … instead of going home … if only I could … if I could tell somebody … if only I had someone to turn to!

And all at once the tears have started pouring down my cheeks and into the beer glass, and the woman with the husky voice quietly rests her hand on my shoulder. The touch was so warm and considerate that I reflexively clasped my hand over hers with relief. A strange torpor had come over me, and when a wave of loneliness and self-pity broke over me, I put up no resistance. I let it wash over me. I wanted to be unhappy. I wanted to be pitied. I wanted to let myself be carried on the wave of sympathy which I felt washing about me. To let it buoy me onwards. To give up struggling. When I looked up I didn't care if everybody saw how unhappy I was. Yes, I wanted everybody to see it. And of course, everybody's eyes were on me. The chatter had turned into a hushed, concerned whisper which murmured in my ears like the babbling of water. The flabby man had come and sat down beside the woman with the clown's mouth. He watched me with this forthright gaze as if he never needed to blink his eyes, and they seemed to be floating in water. Just then I didn't know whether he belonged to the race of men or fish, and I stared at him, transfixed. Powerless. It was as if I couldn't tear my eyes off him, but at that moment the husky voice asked me if I was all right? Said that maybe this wasn't the right place for me.

Actually it is, I said. This is just the place for me. My daughter's sitting in prison just down the road.

Then she took my hand and led me to her flat behind the dining area.

She sat me down on the couch like a child. She took a woollen blanket and laid it over my shoulders. She went to get a foot stool and placed it under my feet. She ministered to me. Yes, ministered. That's the right word. Not because she was pampering me and bringing me this and that, but because she granted me what I was in need of. I sensed this when she went to get me the cup of tea and I said not to worry because she was supposed to be serving customers next door, but without a word she lifted the tea up to my lips and helped me drink as if her job next door didn't belong in this moment, and then I understood that she was ministering to me. She said she'd help me get home and asked where I lived.

I'm just staying at a hotel, I said, and before I knew it I'd started crying again.

There's room at my place if you want to make use of it. But you'll have to look after yourself.

So now you know that I didn't move into some guest house near the prison like I told you over the phone. From then on I slept on the couch in Anna's living room. I went to the hotel right away to pick my things up. Funny! It didn't cross my mind at the time that my decision might be impulsive. I've tried to break myself of the habit of acting impulsively, as you well know. I've got myself into the habit of making decisions purely on the basis of careful deliberation. And it wasn't like me to let my life be thrown off-kilter by a moment's whim. When things of that sort befell me, terror washed over me and in the to-ing and fro-ing which came from being uncertain, it was brought home to me that my impulsiveness was a terrible blunder which couldn't be put right. I felt as if I'd committed a wrong. And was filled with remorse. It was just as if the unswerving path with a sure beginning and definite end-point was a question of morality. But this time I felt no remorse. Actually I became even firmer in my decision to switch lodgings when I entered the hotel. In the hotel, my mind was only half there. It was as if I were coming to a place which I'd never seen before except in a dream and which belonged to another time and another world. When the receptionist handed me the bill I looked almost uncomprehending at the dates and figures precisely recorded there. They were so unreal. Like unintelligible runes, almost. The figures no longer really concerned me. As if they were no longer in my blood. I paid the bill and added a generous tip completely out of the blue, as if to ensure good service in future. And I thought to myself: What am I playing at? Was I completely losing my head for money? I've always known when to pay and when not to. But that's when I discovered that I've acquired an entirely different kind of head for money. A completely different feeling from before. I was buying my way out of this world, a world from which it wasn't possible to buy oneself free with any other currency than money. And my clothes which I put in the suitcases, the jewellery, the shoes, everything which I'd tried to choose with care in spite of all the turmoil when I left Iceland, I now lugged with me like dead things. My soul, which used to reside in these objects, had deserted them. I think it's quite safe to say that this was the last stop in fake time.

I was most relieved when the moment arrived when I could ring for a porter to carry my cases downstairs and out into a taxi so that I could get away as soon as possible. Anna had let me have a key to her flat. The entrance was through a side door at the end of a narrow passageway hardly visible from the street. I had the taxi driver stop there. He dumped my cases on the pavement, took his fare, and drove off. And there I stood all by myself. With three large suitcases full of clothes, and smaller bags with toiletries and other odds and ends in them. Had I stood there waving my arm for all eternity, no porter would have come to help me with it. There was no service to be bought for money. Nor could I demand it, because what had Anna said: You'll have to look after yourself. The person who'd ministered to me in my moment of need had made it crystal clear that I wouldn't be waited on here. I'd have to fend for myself. And my arms, which before would have been waving without a second thought for porters and concierges now struggled with the bags, one after the other, into Anna's house.

And the problem was staring me in the face as soon as I got inside. It didn't need any pointing out to me. Where I was to sleep, in the living-room, there was obviously no wardrobe. The one wardrobe in the flat was in Anna's bedroom. I opened it. A few bits of clothing and three empty clothes-hangers. And as if I had succumbed to fate, I now took everything as signs or pointers. These hangers were meant for me. From now on I'd go around in what three clothes hangers would allow. And so I took nothing but a smooth, plain dress from a case together with two changes of blouse. The suit I was wearing would do most of the time and was appropriate, because a woman's suit is actually a happy disguise for women who are betwixt and between and haven't yet decided whether they're going to cross over a borderline, but outwardly they inspire confidence. Whoever sees a woman in a suit remains unruffled. He doesn't expect this sort of woman to pull any stunts. I didn't even open the other cases. I managed to jam the biggest one under the couch. The other two I put in a little cubby-hole which I found off the kitchen. My coat I hung on a hook by the front door. Then I was fully settled in.

I couldn't get to sleep that night.

I whirled around free of fate in the chaos of a beguiling gulf. Fear and anger like wheels which spun me endlessly round and round. As if I hadn't been here for eight winters at all. Never learnt anything. Never spent time in the forest with troll-women and slept out of doors with wolves, armed only with bow and arrows. The forest had taught me to meet fear face to face. Urthur had sent me into the forest. That's when it was revealed to me that it's the fear which howls, and when I'd overcome it, I spoke the language of wolves. But now I knew that fear has many faces, no less than the goddess does. Where was Urthur sending me now? I was annoyed with her. She knew that I couldn't see the future. I'd have to make do living with presentiments. She lived with certainties. She saw everything before it happened and remembered what never was. But I wasn't allowed to ask her about anything, because she says nothing except of her own will. She's never spoken my destiny. Not even when I was a child in my father's house. I remember that I was playing on the floor when she entered the hall. Everybody fell silent. She stood in a blue-black mantle, embroidered at the shoulders, her black hair like a crown on her head. Her eyes sparkled. I thought at first that this was the goddess herself. She was so mighty. My father lifted me up off the floor. He laughed and held me up in his arms and said:

So then, Urthur, what do you make of my daughter Gunnlöth?

I can hear from the name what part you have in mind for her, Urthur answered.

Urthur took me in her arms. A scent of flowers came from her mantle and she held me so tightly that I've known ever since how blue-black smells.

She looked into my eyes and then pressed me so tightly to her breast that I seemed to hear a swishing sound in my ears.

An eagle is flying overhead, Urthur said.

Then she put me down and I ran back to my father. He was pleased with her answer and counted it a good omen.

And when I feel Urthur is being too strict with me I remember the time she clasped me to her chest. And then I know that I'm fonder of her than of anybody else. I began to grow calm and sensed Urthur's presence close by in my lodge, and I knew then that my anger wasn't aimed at her. It was aimed at my helplessness. At the terror of not understanding. Incomprehension is an affliction. All instruction has the aim of stripping the veil from my eyes so that I might sense the connectedness of all things. So what meaning did Urthur's words contain? Urthur's words were never meaningless. Were they a warning? An omen? Could they have something to do with the choice of king ahead of us?

I thought back over the day my father came to tell us about the new king-to-be. I remembered that day very clearly, but I was trying now to examine the day's events in my mind, to listen in on them in case there had been omens hidden there which naively or arrogantly I had overlooked. Perhaps I'd manage it in the still of the night. Although I wasn't gifted with foresight, Urthur had trained me in the sensitivity which makes people able to sense omens, in a similar way that the harpist can sense with both his ears and his fingers that a string is going to snap. Omens occurred all the time and everywhere in life. They weren't aimed at any person in particular and it was up to everybody to listen out, because they indicated an upset in the order of the universe, that order which both men and gods had to bow to. Whoever was unable to pick up on omens wasn't attuned to life's rhythm. But it wasn't enough to sense omens. You needed to work them out as well. When you've learned to scan sky and earth and know the source of the winds and hear the grass growing, she'd said ... yes, but does anybody learn that in a single life? It's not in my power to strip the veil from your eyes, she would always say. But I knew that she who through lack of vigilance allowed the string to snap apart was not fit to be a priestess. I became downcast as I considered whether such a destiny had been made for me. Had arrogance clouded my mind? I'd been both astonished and proud of myself that day when Urthur asked me to her lodge where my father was sitting. I had never before been present at one of their talks.

Urthur invited me to sit down on the bench beside her. I remember becoming a little anxious when I saw that my father was sitting by a fire. It wasn't the custom for fires to be lit indoors in broad daylight and I asked my father whether he was ill. He said no, but jiggled his shoulders slightly as was his way when he felt words to be of no use, and then said smiling that as long as there existed no remedy for old age, he'd just have to turn the heat on it a bit. I noticed that his hands had aged since I'd last seen him. And the wrinkles on his face had become deeper. My father had been sacrificial priest for a long time, and the gods set their mark on those men who shared knowledge with them. Carved runes into their skin whose interpretation was beyond the power of most.

We'll not worry ourselves about such things, said my father. No-one can thwart what's fated for them. Urthur tells me that you're equal to taking on the role which has been planned for you, and for which you've been trained.

I felt myself flush with joy. Did Urthur look away just then? I remember now that a shadow so faint that it looked more like the omen of a shadow than the shadow itself passed over her face. At the time I put it down to the flickering of the fire, for joy was never denied us. Perhaps my mind hadn't been on worthy things?

But my father continued. He said that a messenger had come from his sister Bestla and delivered the news that King Bor had departed. He had intended the kingdom to pass on to his son Odin when his time was at an end, and Bestla's message went on that we would hallow the choosing of that king the first night of the new year.

I'd never seen Odin but I'd seen my father's sister Bestla at a sun-festival which I'd been allowed to attend as a child. Before I became priestess. I remember thinking her beautiful and admiring her finery. About her neck she wore a golden ring with beads of amber. It was a queen's neck-ring, and I'd never seen a ring more beautiful, except for the one my mother wore. I remember it shooting through my mind that I would now wear my mother's neck-ring the first night of the new year. The ring of the priestess. Were my thoughts tied too much to Gunnlöth, and not the goddess? Bestla had been priestess before my mother and hallowed the choosing of Bor as king, but when they fell in love, she was married to him and moved away because a priestess could be no man's wife. I'd seen King Bor when he came here into the shrine for winter sacrifices and annual assemblies. He was a dark-haired, tall man, but sedate. I knew that he observed his faith and was a just king, and peace had been kept in the land. He and my father had always got on well. And my father said:

Peace has ruled here for a long time and the crops have enjoyed good weather from our king.

And then carried on after a short silence but spoke slowly as if preoccupied:

And no change should come with Odin's rule if the prophecy he received when young is borne out, that his name would be honoured beyond all kings. And Bestla's message went on to say that I should remember that prophecy.

I remember that my heart was filled with laughter, to be allowed to hallow such a king. I also wanted the king I hallowed to realm and rule to be one I found attractive. But I knew that a priestess shouldn't be thinking like this. That's what Urthur had taught me. The king-to-be didn't concern Gunnlöth. A priestess was performing the deed of the goddess, who would take up residence inside me. All the same, I had difficulty driving these thoughts from my mind as my father spoke, saying that we were in a good position for hallowing a king and holding a festival. The goddess had been well-disposed towards us: supplies were plentiful, the barley had flourished, and the sea had been bountiful.

The gold? – asked Urthur, – for the rings and the regal spear?

And my father replied that a lot of gold had been obtained in exchange for the amber we sold. I remember being delighted at this news. We needed a lot of gold. Not only for consecrating kings, but all the time, for gold was the goddess's metal, and objects dedicated to her couldn't be of metals other than gold. Never was the goddess closer to me than when my hands touched the gleaming metal which in her generosity she gave us humans, for gold was flesh of her flesh, bone of her bone. Urthur had told me that in ancient times it had been the teaching of our distant ancestors that metals are the earth's infants and that in the fullness of time all metals became gold, at which point the goddess brought it forth from herself in rivers and lakes. But gold is slow to develop. And no-one can fathom the earth's time. The year which gave us plenty of gold from other lands to the south was a generous one, and I imagined that the regal spear would require a lot of solid gold. The regal spear I was to hallow, which symbolised the power that the goddess gave a king … now I was to engrave that golden spear …

I recall being startled from my thoughts when my father said:

It might be that my powers have begun to ebb. But I've dreamt dreams which I'm unable to interpret.

Then I became uneasy. I'd never heard my father talk like this. Could he be such a shadow of himself that he no longer had faith in his own abilities?

But father, I said, my voice earnest, hasn't the time come for Loki to assist you?

My father didn't look at me, and neither did Urthur. They both stared into the fire until my father said:

It might have.

I don't know why he answered with such thought and hesitation. And now the idea that Urthur's word of warning could have something to do with Loki preyed on my mind. But I didn't know how that could be. Loki had been with my father for eight years and had full command of ancient wisdom and every rune. My father had taught him ancient deeds of gods and men, known only to him. My father himself had said that Loki's gifts were great. He was to become sacrificial priest and mighty sage after my father. Everyone knew that.

My father got up.

Fate will decide.

And added as he looked up from the fire:

Bestla's very keen for Odin to succeed to the kingdom.

It is fitting for a mother to have ambitions for her son, Urthur had said.

I haven't seen him since he was a child. He seemed competitive and unruly.

Kings-to-be often seem like that, said Urthur.

Yes. He must have matured, he's been away among other nations so long. The man must be tested out.

And I remember saying in an undaunted voice:

One who's unworthy won't make it through the clashing crags.

I don't know whether *we'll* make it through the clashing crags. And we've certainly not understood the omens.

The lawyer rang me at around this time. He never asked my reasons for moving out of the hotel.

I'm sitting in his office.

He's telling me about the police interviews.

The two guards in the museum who found Dís said they'd thought she'd broken the glass with her bag. Although admittedly they'd not seen it with their own eyes.

This point was being looked into more closely, said the lawyer, because there's no question of being able to break such strong glass with the bag alone. Not even if all the strength in a young girl's body had been behind the blow. Not even if the bag had been full of stones.

So how's she meant to have gone about it then? – I asked a little impatiently because I didn't quite understand where he was heading with this, but I was left speechless when very calmly he answered:

There are tiny electronic devices for shattering glass which can be concealed in a bag.

It got so quiet in there that I could hear myself breathing.

Absurd, I then said, emphatically, where the hell is Dís meant to have got hold of that sort of device?

That's just it, he said. Such devices are expensive, not the sort of thing petty criminals can get their hands on. It might point to connections.

Connections! It's the terrorist theory.

I've told you already that Dís isn't a member of any political organisation! She doesn't even have a point of view, at least not a thought-out point of view ...

It was at that precise moment that the incident in the living-room came back to me ... the time I thought that the living-room window pane or the crystal bowl must have ...

But I took care not to utter a single word about it. Neither did I bring up the watch. I still didn't know where she got rid of it.

But still, that they should suspect an act of terrorism seemed absurdly paranoid to me, something straight out of a tacky courtroom drama. It was just as if everybody had become caricature criminals from the movies! Dís, a seasoned criminal! Unthinkable! But although I thought it absurd that she should be under this suspicion, I couldn't close my eyes to the fact that the suspicions harboured about these caricatures were real, just as real as the job offer on your desk which I wasn't the least bit able to put from my mind, no matter how hard I tried. It was neither a figment of my imagination nor a delusion, and it threw my mind into total disarray ...

Shouldn't it have been found in her bag then, this electronic device?

It was apparently quite late on that they thought to look in her bag. Or anywhere else. But that won't hold them back from further investigation, if that's what they choose. An investigation of that sort could draw out the custody over a very long period.

But she was caught right away, wasn't she? Where could she have got rid of a device like that?

Actually it doesn't seem possible to me at all that she could have got rid of anything.

So you don't believe this?

No. I've come to think that the right thing would be for me to request a psychiatric assessment. Try to rule out these terrorists.

You might think I'd be glad he'd come to this decision. It's what I'd been pressing for. But now I felt torn in two different directions. It was obvious to me that this was a turning point. But I didn't know my own wavering mind. Either to request a psychiatric assessment at once, as I'd asked at the outset, or to let the investigation run its course. Probably a prison sentence, but wasn't there still a glimmer of hope that she'd be acquitted? Just a glimmer? No, an infinitesimal hope. Shouldn't you fight tooth and nail for your child no matter what? Or was that the mistaken heroism of someone who's losing everything? Wasn't it better to adapt to circumstances and to gain just a little ground? To steer the way things were going yourself? Get this over with as soon as possible without complicating things any more than was necessary? And Gunnlöth? Was she in her right mind? This had got to be a temporary disturbance. If we were lucky, she'd be sentenced to attend some sessions with a psychologist. In the worst case, to some time in hospital. The thread of Dís's fate is in my hands. Where should I hide the end of it: in prison or in hospital?

To play for time and hide the fact I was at a loss, I said:

You once said there was a chance that the Crown Prosecutor might request a psychiatric assessment himself.

That's right.

So perhaps it wasn't in my power to shield her from a psychiatric assessment in any case. Yes, that was my thinking.

I was rather curt with the lawyer. And the way I reacted was unbelievably mean-spirited. I told him that he ought to be the best judge of the matter and that what he decided was likely to be sensible. Yes, that's how I put it. I threw all the responsibility onto him, as if I'd never brought the idea up myself. I regretted my words as soon as they'd left my mouth. Because even if he'd reached this conclusion all by himself and would ultimately bear responsibility for it, I'd requested we follow this course of action at the very beginning, no two ways about it. And now I behaved as if I were going along with a suggestion of his!

He turned away and busied himself with studying his white Venetian blinds. Angled his profile towards me. One of his ears. I don't know what he was expecting to hear with this ear which coiled like a snail shell out from under his untrimmed hair. Some undertone from the depths of my shame, perhaps, because I said nothing out loud. I felt there was no hope of taking my words back because my shame was bottomless and my offence unforgivable. And had to do with others besides just the lawyer. I'd stood up to get out of there when he turned briskly in his chair, looked me in the face, and said:

I'm considering getting in touch with a historian of religion.

I was so distraught that I didn't think it worth the effort of responding to this, holding my course out into the dingy corridor, and on the way down this crumbly old building's chilly stairs, the darkness slipped me the suspicion that I'd condemned Dís to an asylum, and I didn't know whether I'd ever be granted the opportunity – or should I say the mercy – to make amends for my offence, because it was uncertain whether my victim would ever be coming back home from this journey she was on.

I was many leagues beneath the earth.

And my torment consisted of still to be following her.

She said she was none the wiser, despite retracing these past events in her mind. It only made me more depressed about my father, she said. I'd never known him so heavy-hearted before. Of course, we must all have been wishing for a good king. But the testing-out of the king-to-be and the knowledge which he obtained should settle the matter of his fitness … and now Urthur's wisdom sounded in my ears, the things she had taught me long ago, and it was as if she herself had begun her chanting where I lay without sleeping in my lodge, the chant mingling with my thoughts:

You know that no king rules prosperously except in pact with the goddess. Should he not do so, things will go badly. An age will go to ruin and brothers will battle, woman bear no child, cow yield no milk, corn bear no grain. A king must be of godly origin. He must be knowledgeable in ancient runes and ancient wisdom, and shall use them for his own well-being and his kingdom's and to guard against every evil. The deeds of gods and men must he know. So mighty is that ancient wisdom that the one who commands it will become like the gods and it is taught to few. No-one acquires that knowledge except in return for sacrifice, and that sacrifice is a holy mystery. Your father attends to instruction and sacrifice.

And you …

I'd remained with Urthur. My father had left. On leaving he'd taken me in his arms and kissed me on either cheek. He approached me tenderly, and for the briefest moment I thought I detected in his manner the same kind of respect he had always shown my mother. He mourned for her probably more than I had imagined.

Urthur said that a time of preparation would now begin, when all forces would need to be working in harmony.

The goddess will take up residence in you. When the king-to-be has risen like a new moon from the mysteries and sworn his devotion to the goddess with a ring-oath, he will be brought to you.

Everything we do is a sacrifice. Every sacrifice is a repetition of the acts of the gods so that the world might endure. You know that when we sprinkle white mud upon the ash tree we are creating the world afresh. The dews which drop from the branches of the ash make mother earth fertile. As when the horse Hrímfaxi dampens the earth with drops of foam from his mouth every morning. As when the rime which fell of old in days before memory made the waters fertile, and from the deep rose the earth, and out of her muddy womb, at the point where earth and water met, the first creature slithered, which now lies coiled around her. The goddess takes many forms. She is mother earth. She is the cow Authumla who gave all men life and sustenance. The women down in the village who till the fields revere her in that form, and you know that cutting back undergrowth or breaking new earth is not allowed before the cow has hallowed it. You've seen them leading the cow over the land. And the goddess is the fiery wheel itself, which drives in its wagon around the vault of heaven.

Kings are guardians of the rule just as we are. Kings sacrifice themselves so that a world might be made afresh from out of the moist depths before there was anything. As if he were un-made, the king-to-be slithers back into the dark death-womb of mother earth. Out of him, everything is created afresh. As out of the first god to be sacrificed. But his life he finally gets from the goddess. The sacrificial drink which you serve him is the drink of immortality, and your womb, the womb of life. In this way you give of yourself for the life which the goddess gives of herself. With these embraces you hallow the union of king and realm. His power to rule he gets from you.

It was as if the last of Urthur's chanting had been taken up by the wind itself and now I first noticed a gust of wind blowing over the roof and drops of rain starting to fall on the firm thatch roof. The thatch softened as it received the rain, drinking gratefully. It was a soft, repetitive sound which brought me peace and I felt as if the goddess had asked her son, the sky-god, to send a cloud up into the clear evening sky to put my mind at rest. And while the sky-god sprinkled my memories with his drops of rain I managed to get to sleep and in my dream I thought I heard a dog's dull barking in the distance announcing the arrival of strangers, and the king-to-be who I'd never set eyes on in my waking life appeared to me, and he came into my lodge with a playful glint in his eye, his golden hair such a rich profusion of bright shades that I don't know whether to compare it to the sun or to fire. Then I saw that it was Loki.

My fair girl was sent for psychiatric assessment. As I requested. That was where the first ruling was passed. And since I'd requested it, the outcome had inherently to be to my advantage. She had to be suitably disturbed, my daughter, enough to get her off a prison sentence. But not seriously ill. I needed to have a word with the psychiatrist to that effect. This was going to be a delicate balancing act.

I was summoned for an interview with the psychiatrist. Opted to walk, even though it was a very long way. The hospital building could be seen a long way off. And grew bigger the closer I got to it. I headed towards it without looking around me. I'd set off too early. I wasn't keeping such good track of time as I used to. I started thinking about where I should wait. That's when I came across the garden. I don't know whether it belonged to the hospital, but from then on it became a habit of mine always to ready myself for interviews with the psychiatrist in this garden. It was very handy for mental patients' mothers prior to going in for interviews in the knowledge that their child was driven to this place on a regular basis, guarded in the security of a police car. Because the child is under strong suspicion of a major crime. Under suspicion of planning to steal a national treasure.

I'd walked a long way along a tall monotonous hedge when it suddenly opened up into this garden. I was so weary that anyone seeing me from behind as I tottered along the gravel pathway between the trees must have seen an old woman. My whole body was aching. My legs could hardly carry me any further. And just as I was about to start looking around for a bench, the avenue opened out onto a circular lawn surrounded by trees, and in the middle stood a large oak tree. And beneath the tree was a bench. I sighed like an old woman as I sat down. Stretched out my weary legs. I didn't pay much attention to my surroundings. Felt out of place. Unused to hanging around in gardens. Only took in the colours. The sickly, pallid greens of the shrubs. A long way from coming out in leaf all over. Interspersed with winter brown. But then I began to examine the way the heavy branches of the oak tree hung down over my head. Like the helmet of invisibility from the fairy tales. That suited me fine. I wouldn't have minded being invisible. The guise of a bird would have been gratefully accepted as well. Why not turn into a mother eagle? Then I could carry my young in my talons up to a high mountain ledge, far up out of the clutches of men. Or an owl, who could let its eyelids drop slowly shut and doze with indifference inside the stout trunk of this oak? Not this weary old woman. It was going to take me a long time to get my youthful vigour back, become my old self. I had the suspicion that my heart wasn't in it. Didn't want to be in the present moment, and it sent a chill down my spine when I saw the old woman. It was just as if my thoughts had conjured her up, in some mysterious way caused her to materialise. But she wasn't alone. They must have come off some side-path, quiet and slow and so ancient that they barely have the strength to lift their feet from the ground on this stroll of theirs. They walk hand-in-hand, shoulder to shoulder, leaning against each other like this to keep themselves going, an old couple who show so much concern for one another that neither dares to back off or pass away. Knowing that in that case, the other would fall. Each has become an unflagging walking stick for the other. And so they need to live on for ever. The paradox of love? – I thought as I watched them walk off hand-in-hand until they vanished from my sight into the undergrowth and I could only make them out as two old trees of which none knows from which roots they rise.

I don't know how long I sat there under the oak tree. The paradox of love? And because my brain is old and weary and dull, this passed muster with me, but there was a wistful sorrow there too. Under the bench. At the earth's deepest layer. It gnawed at the root, invisible and silent. Sorrow doesn't have a language.

When the squirrel runs over my foot I'm jolted back again into my past, which was then the present. And it suddenly strikes me that Dís hadn't mentioned the squirrel. But it was meant to run up and down the ash tree though. I remember distinctly because when I did it in school I'd never seen a squirrel. You remember things which take you by surprise. I couldn't work out what a squirrel was doing there in an Icelandic poem. Looked intently at the squirrels which ran up and down the tree-trunks in the garden. Why hadn't Dís mentioned the squirrel? I was suddenly troubled. I felt the squirrel mattered. Had she forgotten it? But then I pulled myself together. This squirrel was real. On my instep I could still feel the gentle but slightly unpleasant scrape of its claw. Came back to myself as if the squirrel had spanned some gap between insanity and reason. Between past and present. I got up abruptly. Obviously the squirrel couldn't settle the matter of whether or not she was crazy.

I followed a gravel path towards the hospital building. On my route there was a pond with raised edges. No swans on the pond. I sat down at its edge. On the bare ground. Having become a woman of three clothes-hangers, having become dulled and unfussed by dirt, defenceless, with neither a silk scarf nor a water-tight opinion to shelter behind during the interview before me. Just followed the magical ball of twine high and low without knowing where it would end. I looked at the grass. Picked a few blades. Scrunched them up in my palm. They were soft. For a second I felt their thirst for life and absent-mindedly stretched my hands down into the pond and filled my palms with water. Made a beaker out of them. It wasn't before I'd lifted it up to my lips that I came back to myself. I seemed to get a whiff of stagnant ditch-water. Needless to say, the water was black with silt. As if all that was left was for me was to go and kill myself here with contaminated water! It can prove fatal, getting distracted. No wonder the swans were nowhere to be seen. I couldn't see to the bottom of this pond. There was nothing living here. No fish would have been able to find its way around this mire. How the hell could it have crossed my mind to call this a pond? All was not as it seemed in this hospital's paradise. I got to my feet and carried on. On closer inspection I saw that the brown patches on the trees of the avenue weren't normal. These weren't trees which had still to come into leaf as I'd thought. These were conifers. They should have been green through the winter but were brown and didn't look long for this world. As if they'd been sprinkled with drops of poison.

The psychiatrist greeted me with a firm handshake. He was short and stout. One of those distinguished grey-haired types in a white coat. Cut out for the part if it had been a role in a film. He sat down at his desk and offered me a seat opposite. Started leafing through papers, and I tried to stand firm, cautioning myself to act naturally. Called on many years' practice in self-discipline. Just make sure you're cool-headed and sensible and talk clearly about nothing in particular. Exercise my concerns in moderation in order to gain the doctor's confidence. In order to distance myself from the notoriety of that most incurable of all incurables: hysteria. Whatever you do, show no symptom of hysteria. And my earnest gaze didn't falter, nor did the expression on my face change when he looked up ready to begin the interrogation – interview, I mean – by which point he'd drawn an invisible blind over his face. No expression. A professional expression, I thought to myself straight off. I wasn't meant to know what he was thinking. But it was also a clever trick. This sort of impersonal expression was meant to let me know that I wasn't being judged. It was meant to arouse a feeling of trust in me with the aim of getting me to draw back the blind from over my soul. I saw through it. As if I didn't know that psychiatrists are detectives who snoop about the mind's alleys and pitch-dark passageways!

He began very casually by asking whether he would also get a chance to meet the girl's father for a talk. Was this done deliberately to bring out the anger in me? Because when I said that he couldn't make it, I was filled with a sudden and unexpected anger. As if I too wouldn't have liked to stay at home without a care in the world like some I could mention, steering the Mercedes along well laid-out streets in accordance with the orderly and easy-to-follow signalling of the traffic-lights. Instead of here, answering questions about our private life, though without understanding the meaning in my own words. I certainly spoke in normal language, in clear, well-balanced sentences as I gave the same old account of our situation. And yet I was seized by the discomforting feeling that the man in the white coat was an interpreter, simultaneously translating my words into the legally recognised language of insanity. In this case, Gunnlöthese. Perhaps the words' meaning was reversed entirely? All I knew was that I was exposing my child's shocking madness, where delusions of grandeur and sexual fantasies were simmering together in a single pot. A more noxious drink, perhaps, than even the cooks themselves can stomach.

And then the conversation took a different turn. He asked whether I'd had reason to believe that my daughter thought she had the power to break things!

The power to break things?

That stopped me in my tracks. My sense of security vanished. No, not because the question took me by surprise, but because that was the very phrase going through my own mind. I'd been thinking in exactly the same way. As if she had the power to break things. But she broke nothing that time. It was just the sound of her voice. The time she said she didn't mean to break anything. Not that time. The thing I'd kept silent from the lawyer.

Poltergeist, he then said. Asked whether I'd ever heard of it. Said that it sometimes happened to certain people that things around them started breaking or moving out of place without any visible cause.

Now I regained control over myself. To be honest, I'd had enough and I answered a little irritably that I'd seen a film about the phenomenon but that I for my part didn't believe in the supernatural, demons and spirits and all that sort of nonsense.

Then in a controlled voice, his face barely moving, he said that explanation of the phenomenon was hardly to be sought in the cinema. It was clearly not supernatural, although indeed difficult to research scientifically. Many psychiatrists and psychologists thought that the poltergeist phenomena were the result of energy unleashed inside the person themselves … especially under stress or if there tended to be tension in the home … teenagers seemed more readily affected than others …

And it was perfectly obvious! It's no wonder I'm scared of teenagers … so it was an energy … an awesome energy … you never know what they might get up to. Their bodies are natural electronic devices. No need for it to have anything to do with terrorist activities.

When I asked whether this was considered to be a serious mental illness, and he assured me that it was usually temporary and even took the teenager in question by surprise and could be most unpleasant for them, I considered whether I ought to tell him about the incident at home in the living-room. Even though I would perhaps be making too big a thing out of it? Hysteria. But if Dís really needed help? Shouldn't I tell him about it? But I was hesitant about making my daughter into material for psychiatrists. What exactly was I trying to do to her?

A person who is arguing two sides of the same question finds it increasingly difficult to make his mind up. His actions are slowed. His tongue as well. He disappears into silent, unfruitful dialogues with himself, trotting out questions and answers at will and triumphing when he brings a crushing defeat upon himself in the debate.

Perhaps deep down I wanted to ask him for help when I made up my mind to tell him about it. Maybe in the hope that in the language of insanity, my sick little narrative might be normal.

At the time I thought that this was just one of Dís's tantrums. This refusal to back down which was so ungovernable. No way of getting her into the habit of using rational arguments in discussions. I tried to teach her that reason and self-control were the prerequisites for voicing her opinion and kept things peaceful. Not this endless squabbling. I was afraid of her lack of restraint – for her own sake, I said – because slowly but surely she drove others to defend an opposite point of view. She didn't make the connection. Unearthly, splitting the atom, she said. God only knows I wasn't defending the world's armaments! Just who does, exactly? But still a quarrel started because she managed as she always did to twist everything into an accusation against us, as if we were to blame for all of this and I remember that the quarrel sparked off spontaneously, inside me, somewhere in my belly, and word sparked off word and hardened and broke out of me like a hail-storm and I said that she should stop running us down as if we were responsible for everything that was going wrong in the world and when I told her that nuclear power just wasn't the issue, she threw herself onto her head. In the middle of the living-room. I thought I heard a crack. Not a shattering sound. Nothing broke. I thought a crack must have appeared in the big pane of the living-room window. Or the crystal bowl. But couldn't find a break anywhere. I still don't know what it was that cracked.

I screamed at her of course. Asked her what the hell she was up to, and she answered:

Just trying to understand you.

But I didn't tell the doctor that the thing which had stuck in my mind most of all was the sight of her the wrong way up. As if she'd thrown herself in an instant into some dreadful monster world where everything human had reached its end. Terrified, I covered my eyes. I'd suddenly been jolted over the boundary of what was credible, and still had my hands over my eyes when Dís walked out, whispering in my ear slowly and clearly with this eerie tone – so sure of victory – in her voice, jangling in my ears like words of a prophecy, and I told the doctor that she'd said:

I didn't break anything for you. Not this time.

And suddenly I realised that I'd exposed us both. Forgotten

myself in the story. I should have kept quiet. For I realised that this incident might be understood differently to how I thought. It couldn't be ruled out that Dís had intentionally concealed an omen in her words, a threat pointing forwards in time precisely to the event in the museum and which I might perhaps have been able to make out had I listened. The words *this time* are taking on an altered significance in my mind, so sinister that they scare me. Could she not just as well have been referring to a man-made electronic device? Might this not lend support precisely to her suspected links with a terrorist organisation? Mightn't it be thought that she'd got mixed up in something and had been getting some point of view across when she broke the glass in the museum?

But could this lack of restraint be so fearsome that solid matter shattered in the face of the energy which was unleashed? What then? Is that kind of lack of restraint a point of view, then, which the hearing of rational people doesn't pick up? A wordless point of view? Raised at wits' end, out of fear and pain?

A shudder ran through me when it struck me what Dís must have seen from her upside-down position. When she threw herself onto her head and looked at me. I'd never considered it before. And I almost wished for the indifference and deafness to voices once more. That I'd never heard this … but my thoughts just then were composed of many voices because it was impossible for me to predict whether this would tip the scales towards criminal behaviour or insanity.

But he'd as yet made no mention of what was weighing most heavily on my mind … the only possible evidence of the state her mind was in … but I shouldn't have thought it! He picked it out of the air of course. I'd become so distraught that I felt my thoughts would surely be carried to him on a current of air, like Urthur's unspoken words on the breeze.

He started speaking about the story, obviously. Asked whether she'd told me the same thing. I said that she had, and he said something about it being remarkable! That it was quite unusual for sufferers of wayward imaginations – he used some technical term of course, but that was his drift – to be so consistent and organised in their thinking, almost realistic in their fantasy. In it she'd built up a whole nation with a rigid social order: with a king, a sacrificial priest and a farmer class, trade with amber and gold. Gold and green forests. Peace. All of a sudden he was talking like a promoter of tourism selling me a summer holiday and for a second, a mournful note crept into his voice, barely noticeable. From what I could hear he was yearning to go there himself! But I feigned a lack of interest. I was by no means keen for this land to be opened up to tourists.

He finally drew back the blind from his face entirely and asked amicably but with no particular interest, as if he were enquiring out of politeness after the woman next door:

Who was she actually, this Gunnlöth?

I answered without hesitating:

Odin stole the art of poetic invention from her.

And I was filled with a weary anger. Why was I forever having to explain who this Gunnlöth was? The one who … I'd never had the least bit of interest in her. That much is certain! I tried to hide my anger and he remained silent for some time. I didn't break the silence. He could adjourn proceedings to think things over as far as I was concerned. To the end of the century if need be. I was dreading his words, because no mother enjoys receiving confirmation of what she wants to avoid knowing, that perhaps there has been some madness in her child all along. And that they will be declared more unwell than she hopes.

It was at about this point that I felt I was losing my grip completely. Soon I'd be forced to face up to the fact that I was going to get nothing more out of Dís than this bizarre story and that all my efforts to direct her down routes more congenial to me would be to no effect. That I would have to admit I was weak and had been beaten, and I would be faced with the obvious fact that I was no more in control of this madness of hers than I'd been in control of her sanity.

On my motionless drift through the upper air it's hard to think back to my jumbled emotions from this time. And I have to admit that they become unreal when I look at Dís between these sturdy bridge piers sitting on either side of her. She's like a big, calm river which flows onwards, self-contained and indifferent. She doesn't look over at me. She's already made arrangements for me. Has a new role lined up for me. And all of a sudden I've started to understand how difficult it's going to be. To fill that role I'll have to grant the fish wings and get gills for the eagle. And I reflect on how far it is to the ninth world and how easy it is to imagine that the ether is just an unpeopled waste, empty, solely because my vision can make out nothing through the window except this endlessness. And yet I know that claims have been staked to these territories. Men have roamed here with fire and wielded their hammer, and an invisible destiny is being carried to us on the currents of the air. I don't know how many feet above the earth we are. It's a long time since the aerial driver reported to us. The earth, too, is invisible in these deep seas. But we believe we know it's there … that it's not just our imagination even though at the moment it's like land waiting to rise up afresh … we create it from what we've experienced and from the moist depths … a world is created afresh … *when we sprinkle white mud upon the ash tree, we are creating the world afresh* … Urthur is singing in my ear … *sacrifice ourselves so that the world might be formed afresh* … let ourselves be torn limb from limb while Dís creates her realm.

I dreamed the events of the coming day. Woke up late. It had stopped raining and the ground had dried in the mild autumn breeze. Everything was calm. As often before, the light of day drove away the thoughts of a sleepless night. I went into the pantry and got myself milk and bread. As I drank the cool milk I felt I'd been making too much of an omen. Forgotten the knowledge I'd acquired in the forest. And yet Urthur had told me when I came back strong and bold from the forest that the gloomy forest's knowledge would live on in me forever. Urthur had taught me such a lot. My trouble was remembering it and using it to my advantage. Remembering that it's the fear which howls. Remembering that fear takes many forms, none of which is any stronger than the others. The brightness of the dream was still in my mind. Now I felt strong and fearless, and I thought fondly of the wolves. I had nothing to fear from a king-to-be. Speaking as I could the language of wolves, I'd surely also be able to speak the language of men.

When I'd eaten I walked up onto the flat rock on the south side of the hill where the landscape was unremarkable but from where the secret path ran between where we women lived and my father's houses. From the rock the path dived down into a cleft which our distant ancestors had carved out at the dawn of time. Whoever knew his way along this secret path vanished from the sight of men as if he'd stepped into the rock-face. Then an avenue of trees began which wound its rambling way to my father's hall. From this point on, no-one who was uninitiated could see me because ancient knowledge determined that a damp mist appeared to those who drew near, although we could see far and wide. And to those who lived here, this path was as clear as day.

I took care not to step on the sacred signs which had been carved onto the rock in ancient times. They invoked the goddess and warded off evil. Here on the edge of the shrine there was need for strong protection. The sun-sign was largest, but further up on the rock coiled the serpent. Beakers were set into the face of the stone so that the rock could receive the rain when the sky god wet it. And the sky god's hammer and the double-bladed axe. In spite of the signs and the mist which concealed us, you had to be on your guard in this place. This was a boundary. Not a peaceful holy place like by the ash tree. I didn't generally linger alone here for long, but on this occasion I'd been driven here by a premonition that the dog's barking in my dream heralded news. And I hadn't been standing long when I saw the trees by my father's hall move and I knew someone was coming. And suddenly everything sprang into motion. The trees started to bend in the calm weather as if a sorcerous gale had suddenly been conjured up, but a white gust of wind showed between the branches, its bright mane floating up on end as if the winged horse Skinfaxi himself were on his way, and my heart, too, took wing inside my chest and soared with joy, for I knew then that it was Loki. My childhood friend. My best friend. No-one ran with so light a foot as he did. I rushed off to meet him. He'd made it into the cleft when we reached each other and I ran into his arms. With peals of laughter he swung me round in whirling circles until my head spun. Then he kissed me on both cheeks.

Loki, have you come with news?

When Loki saw how impatient I was, he acted so out of breath that he couldn't manage a single word. He started huffing and puffing heavily like a bear, barely inching forwards, his lithe and nimble body in an instant heavy and lumbering, and I fell unprompted into our childhood game. Merrily, full of warmth and compassion, I took the heavy paw, placing it over my shoulder and led the bear up the cleft in the rock and out onto the meadow where the seedy dandelion heads spread themselves out like linen washed white and we sat down there. He lay with his head in my lap and I stroked him like a vexed and worn-out bear cub, merriment jostling with anticipation inside me. And I have to admit that my spine tingled! For all I could tell he would change form before I knew it and spring up agile as a wolf. Or a hare. Loki was a clever mimic and made a game of switching himself into absolutely any guise. As a child I was sometimes seized by too intense an excitement and even terror at this game of his, for in my active imagination he could easily appear other than he was. But if he saw that he was scaring me he packed the game in at once and appeared back to me. Looked on me with bright, gentle eyes to calm me down. Then I could see that it was only Loki. I could always be sure that Loki himself wouldn't change. It had pained me to part from him when I moved to Urthur's and I couldn't understand how I'd be able to survive not seeing Loki every day like I was used to. We'd grown up like brother and sister and he'd always kept me amused with his quick and lively spirit and funny quirks. No-one was funnier or better-looking than he was, and no-one kinder to me. He did what I wanted in everything. But I still hadn't fully grasped that it didn't really matter to me and Loki if we were apart. As before, our thoughts were as one and we kept nothing hidden from each other. Messages passed between us in dreams by night and on the breeze by day. And whenever we saw each other, the blue sky of childhood reigned. With Loki nearby I didn't need to be afraid that shadows cast by omens might darken my thoughts. I looked down at the dense and delicate hair of the lashes over his half-closed eyes and saw that he'd stopped being a bear. He was just Loki.

I knew you would come, I said. I dreamed about you last night.

And I dreamed about you, he answered.

But you've got some news for me even so.

95

Are you frightened, he asked, holding my hand tightly, and I didn't need to ask what he meant. I knew at once that Loki had come to put my mind at rest.

Sometimes, I said, but I know that the goddess will take possession of my mind and body.

He's still with Baugi across the river, but he's expected very soon.

Have you seen him? – I asked.

After eight winters with my father studying ancient wisdom, Loki could obtain knowledge by routes closed to others. In an instant he could switch form and travel vast distances on his errands, or on those of others. I'd once heard my father say that Loki's gift was so great that he could never conduct himself too carefully. I knew that ancient knowledge had to be handled with care if it was to be of benefit to the knower. I also knew that causing harm was the last thing on Loki's mind, although an impatience to put my mind at rest had perhaps governed his journey to Baugi's on this occasion.

What's he like? – I asked.

A dumb bum, boastful, Loki answered. He all but drove me away with his hot air.

That's not true!

No.

Is he straight and supple? Well-built?

Wonderfully built. Although not as handsomely as I am!

I smiled, knowing that the man who was as fair to look at as Loki didn't exist. When I was little I had no doubt that I would be given to Loki in marriage. Before I knew that I'd become a priestess. A priestess can be no one man's to have and to hold. That would be just as absurd as the sun shining on only one person. The sun shines on all alike and decides herself when to shine and when not to. That's why my mother and father weren't married even though they loved each other. And a priestess didn't think about a king-to-be as a man whose faults and flaws she could forgive. She had to make demands of him so that peace and justice should reign among the people and that weather should favour the crops. That's why I had asked no questions other than those which it was right to ask about a king-to-be. I would share a bed with him as priestess. Not as Gunnlöth. The goddess herself will take possession of my mind and body and lead the king-to-be to the source of the mysteries and charge him with the power of sun and earth.

I was keen to know more about the coming king and I asked Loki:

What did he talk about?

Loki remained silent for a while and closed his eyes. He took hold of one of my hands and I studied his soft white hands, the long and delicate fingers and well-kept nails. Then he spoke.

Most likely he weaves his own fame with words.

I smiled. You didn't need to travel in shapes other than your own to know that. And I pushed Loki's head from my lap and lay on my belly beside him. The dandelion seeds brushed against my cheek like someone lightly stroking the side of your face goodbye. The fragrance of the undergrowth was steadily fading, and my eyes searched further up onto the heath where the awesomely beautiful expanses of violet autumn heather covered the heath like a bold song in praise of death. In this violet-coloured song I sensed the omen of a peril which nothing would be able to avert unless all powers were in tune with each other to wake everything up afresh, and I turned towards Loki and said:

Bor, his father, was a very devout man.

I think that Odin has all the abilities a king needs, said Loki.

Yes, I said, feeling that Loki wanted me to shake off my anxiety. And I wanted to as well. I wanted to enjoy the time I spent together with Loki. And so, light in tone, I began to list everything that I knew kings needed to be able to do:

He's well accomplished. He knows how to handle a sword and throw a spear, sit a horse and chase down wild beasts …

Loki took over from me:

He's travelled widely and has been among other nations … seen such a lot …

So have you, I said.

Me?

97

Yes, you've seen more than any king and travelled vast distances and know all the worlds.

Then Loki laughed, knowing that I was planning to ask him to sing. I sat up and remembered how often Loki's songs had danced about the sinking autumn sun and awoken a promise of new life. And Loki gave in to what I wanted like he used to when we were inseparable and owned everything in common: flower, lamb and sun, and he turned himself into one guise after another, in songs just as much as in games, and it wasn't until later that I understood that his games were real life from other times, and his songs memories from other life-spans. That he was one of the few who carried inside him the quick of everything because nothing that had once been had ever died off in him. He remembered the life of stones and plants and of every animal. Not only did he know the life of both sexes, but also the life that was lived before every living thing separated into its opposite parts. Memory could stop the whirling wheel at any moment and put a song on his lips.

> I was drizzle
> that drummed on the snake,
> a fashioned flintstone.
> An ash I was
> on an empty shore,
> woman's son and his sister.
> The wolf's father …

The song petered out in laughter as if he'd been reciting funny verses and he put his arms around my neck and pulled my head down so that my lips touched the top of his head and I kissed him on the forehead as I had done as a child while the song soared from his chest and I was in no more doubt now than before that Loki had known me in all these life-spans. And his song kindled a poem in my chest, and word kindled from word in me because I wanted to be the snake which he drizzled on, the fire which he lit, and a tree-trunk on the shore by his side. I couldn't conceive of my being absent from Loki's memories.

Before Loki went I dragged him home with me to the kitchen to get him some whey to drink. At first he declined but I pressed him because I wanted to have him with me longer. And Loki bowed to my will like he always did. Then I went on with him to the flat rock and talked about the new year sacrifice and how much I was looking forward to it. I would be sitting in the high seat at my father's side. With the gold-embroidered band around my forehead and the most beautiful ring around my neck. And the new king on the other side of me. The poets would entertain us all with stories and songs to the accompaniment of the harp, the girls would dance, and my relatives would come flocking from all around. There would be an abundance of food on the tables and the drinking-horns would brim with foaming ale.

I parted from him down from the houses and watched as he ran over the rock towards the hidden path until he vanished down into the surface of the rock.

When I turned to walk home I caught a glimpse of Urthur by her lodge on her way towards the door. The door was open as if she'd only looked outside briefly and gone no further than the yard. From there she could see me and Loki.

And her thought brushed against my ears on the breeze as she disappeared inside:

Don't forget that you're a priestess!

Am I never to be left in peace?

I've had it up to here with Urthur. Dís was right, the time she said that she's always turned up everywhere. Like a cat, she said, if memory serves me right. If a person knows something, then they should say what they know. Not go creeping along the walls in this long black cloak. I've begun to view her as my competitor, although I suspect that I'm no match for her. I catch myself trying to see her in my mind's eye, to pull her closer so that I can read her expression and her behaviour, and feel as if she's giving me clues or setting riddles for me like in the treasure hunt ... but hers are tough riddles to solve ...

Morning's here. Drowsy. Bleary-eyed. I wouldn't have been able to say whether I'd slept well or badly. That odd state which comes from the body sleeping while the mind stays awake beneath some indistinct burden. It *is* also rather gloomy in the kitchen, of course. And it's murky grey outside, but that's not it. It's always gloomy in Anna's kitchen because the kitchen's at the back of the building and looks onto the yard. You can access the kitchen directly from the dining area. One might get the idea that the place used to be a flat with decent front rooms and that Anna's flat had perhaps been the bedrooms, or even a maid's quarters with its own entrance. I don't know. I've never asked. The kitchen table is just a small, two-man table. Or should I say, two-woman.

We're sitting there, drinking our morning coffee.

Anna, directly opposite me at the table, is scrutinising my face as if she senses that there's something particular on my mind, her look so artless that it verges on being intrusive. And I've stopped wearing make-up as well. I'm so naked in the morning ... I would never have dreamed that I was to get so laid back about my appearance ... I always held back from asking whether you noticed the crease between my eyebrows at all ... didn't want to draw it to your attention ... but you won't miss it when we land in a while ... it's got deeper, I think, but otherwise I've stopped noticing it in the mirror ... it's become so familiar to me, and actually I mustn't lose it or the bags under my eyes. For I feel as if Anna reads my thoughts in these wrinkles. She peers silently into my face. Her unruly hair is mottled from countless rinses. It sticks up in the air and winds about her head like a joke halo. I don't know how old Anna is and it doesn't occur to me to ask about something so trivial. But I suspect her hair makes her face look old, and I try to picture her with a different look, with that close cropped hair standard among the middle-aged, for example, regarded as the natural choice in the world up there when you realise it's literally the only means left to conjure forth some trace of youth, but when I look into her eyes I can see that it's not in my power to give her any look. Anna isn't under my control. She doesn't pity me. That's why I'll carry a mark on my shoulder to the end of my days where her hand touched me, and I know that I'll open my mouth before I know what I'm doing and confide my anxieties in her.

We sip at our coffee. We've got plenty of time because Anna doesn't open the pub before around midday. A clattering sound drifts back to us from the dining area. The lad who helps her out in the mornings is stacking the chairs up on the tables so that he can mop the floor. He does the washing up and runs various errands for her so that she can take it easy in the mornings. Anna says that a while back she would have been able to sleep until midday. That she can no longer manage it. That's getting old for you, she says; as the long hours you spend asleep start to shorten, Providence makes it up to you by stretching out your waking hours. When I was a teenager I could have slept my life away. Seemed never to be able to wake up.

No-one can mention a teenager without me flinching in response like someone found guilty of a crime. As if the word itself were a piece of evidence proving my guilt.

So then? – Anna says. What's on your mind?

And the words pile out of me:

This peculiar story she's telling … that Gunnlöth's a priestess … the incarnation of a goddess who ranks over all the gods. And that she grants the king … Odin … the authority or power to rule by giving him a drink of immortality and sleeping with him … with a sacred marriage as it's apparently called …

I stuttered and hiccuped, seemed barely able to repeat this.

… that she's actually the state itself, with power, truth and justice on her side because the goddess apparently preserves the law of heaven and earth and all creation and because no-one can become king unless he acquiesces to this law and swears her an oath … and no-one can get her to drop it … not even me …

Anna burst out laughing her deep laugh, so husky it was like she had a whole cigarette factory in her throat.

I hope she's a better state than the one we have to put up with.

This laughter hurt me. Even though I know that Anna views everything in the same way, and that crimes get her no more worked up than sausages in a pot do.

Anna, how can you treat this as a joke?

Then she took my hand as if I were a child, leaned across the table and said, smiling:

I'm not joking. I mean it seriously. You'll see that when you've understood that being serious is a far more dangerous disease to catch than laughter. Life threatening.

Anna, this is so puzzling. This story she's telling …

Puzzling! Doesn't sound like it to me!

It's so preposterous. I'm … I'm considering whether she's actually seriously …

I hesitated. And the final word was just a whisper:

… insane.

I'd said it. Insane. Now there was no turning back. But I'd never have been able to say this out loud to anyone other than Anna. I waited anxiously for an answer. And now I wanted to hear her laugh this off as absurd, be it for no other reason than to comfort me, but she answered:

That's a possibility.

I sank down in my seat. This woman, I thought, never relieves me of my pain and yet there's nowhere I want to be but here.

At least, it's more reasonable to believe that a woman's disturbed if she sings her own praises. Because only by playing ourselves down are we normal.

That sort of sarcasm isn't appropriate in this case, I'm afraid Anna.

Is that so. So why's she meant to be insane, then?

It's all make-believe. I know that much.

Really?

Yes, the story of the mead of poetry is one everybody knows from school. And Gunnlöth was most certainly not a priestess. And everything she says about Loki ... puzzling ... strange ...

Then Anna got up and walked over to the kitchen window and looked out while I emptied myself of this torrent of words:

She's going too far. This is so absurd. Too absurd to be dismissed as a clever ploy to fool a judge. There's no cause for such wild invention unless your imagination isn't well. And if it's meant to be a practical joke, then that sort of joke isn't normal either. Jokes are just like madness, Anna. No matter what you might say. Something in a person's character which bubbles up out of them if they don't watch themselves. (Yes, I permitted myself to say this to her, always having thought it to show great inanity, being entertaining in public.) So it all boils down to the same thing. Whether Dís was doing it deliberately or not, her mode of thinking wasn't normal. No, it was quite utterly absurd. What nonsense! No, no-one goes to such lengths to act crazy unless they're ... yes, unless they really are crazy.

Anna remained silent for such a long time that I started to mind. She stood stock-still at the window and I remember thinking that the view couldn't exactly have been captivating her. The window looked out onto the back yard where Anna and her neighbours' dustbins took pride of place. Anna's dustbins so full of rubbish and waste from the pub that the dustmen couldn't keep up with it, the bins always half-open, the lids balanced on the topmost layer of rubbish until plastic rubbish bags which cats poked around in started lining up around the bins. She stood there with the empty coffee mug dangling at her side like a handbag, her index finger curled around the handle. Seemed to have forgotten herself. As if the whole of my lecture had shot straight past her and into the rubbish bins.

Maybe it had all gone past her. Or perhaps there was nothing more to be said. She rinsed her mug under the tap. Without washing-up liquid. She wasn't overly concerned with hygiene, Anna, she didn't fuss over things. She kept the mugs on a mug-tree which stood on the kitchen table. And racks and mug-trees weren't for show with her as they are with people who adorn their kitchens with objects that are old and quaint. Anna used these things purely because she had no top cupboards. Most of what she owned was old and tatty. The steadiest customers in Anna's pub were unemployed, and a person making their living off the unemployed isn't going to lead a life of milk and honey themselves. My thoughts turned of their own accord to my own kitchen, and I started comparing it with the lack of comfort here. The lack of comfort which at one time I'd dreaded more than judgement day.

And we both remained silent while Anna hung her mug up on the mug-tree. It was as if rinsing off the mug were a sacred ritual which mustn't be interrupted. Next she dried her hands and only then did she turn to me and say as if we hadn't been on the topic of madness at all:

So tell me: who was she, this Gunnlöth, seeing as you know her so well?

And I spoke without thinking. From old habit:

Odin stole the art of poetic invention from her.

Yes, yes, okay, he stole it from her. That's all very well. But that tells us nothing about her. Who was she? Look, if she's the star of this show, then everything should revolve around her, shouldn't it? Not some walk-on role.

A walk-on role! I practically burst out laughing. This is what she said about the god himself! But Anna was deadly serious. Her gaze so unswerving that it reminded me of Dís. As she's become. Nowhere to run. She meant to get an answer.

Who was Gunnlöth?

Giving Anna an answer required staring in the face what I'd

known all along. But not been able to say. Not yet. I saw only that Anna was pushing me – unable to swim – out into the deep, where I was forced to dive for an answer and there was no way to make it to safety over the surface of the water on a respectable breast-stroke. Let alone a doggy paddle.

To be honest I don't know whether I was playing for time or confirming that my memories of what I'd been taught at school about Gunnlöth and the mead of poets were correct when I strode off to the Royal Library to take out a book of Norse mythology. Both, probably. Although it was really Anna who was prodding me towards the books. The Royal Library was in the other direction. Looking at it from Anna's, I mean. And in relation to the prison. The prison was to the left and this time I went to the right. On a bus into town. In my handbag was a letter of recommendation for the library which I'd plucked up the courage to get for myself at the embassy. It wasn't possible to take books out otherwise. So I'm to some extent justified in saying that on this journey I was on public business. Got off the bus at Rådhuspladsen and walked down to the Canal. I walked slowly and calmly, some sort of stubbornness in my legs which I could do nothing about, and my mind slightly feeble as if I felt it hardly worth the effort of thinking any longer. Felt as if I was going to the library to receive a verdict on Dís's mental well-being. And that the verdict of the psychiatrist would merely be a formality.

There was the library. A grand building. I'd never been inside, of course. I hung back. I – who was used to walking with authority into any institution where I had business to take care of, and apologising to no-one for my existence – became all of a sudden shy of this building, like a schoolgirl. I tried to recall what it had been like walking into the National Library in Iceland for the first time when I was a teenager. I don't remember. Perhaps it felt like this. I wasn't shy otherwise … well, maybe as a teenager. I hadn't been a shy child. There was no wind. Used this as an excuse to walk a little further. The Canal ahead of me. A boat. A sightseeing trip. To be able to just sail along this canal, not a care in the world. The surface so still. The only movement, ripples from the boat. No danger of coming into contact with this water. You just sail onwards as a spectator. No churning from strong currents to shake your insides up. The body sixty-seven percent water. That's the right limit. Neither more nor less if you're to be well-balanced. Life or death. You carry both inside you. We're really little other than containers for water. But how heavy the remaining percentage of me was. Thought I'd never get myself going. I turned back to the library. A good number of people about. But there's plenty of space here and people don't seem to be in a hurry. Maybe because they don't have to elbow their way forwards like in the shopping and office districts. The library steps are old and stately. I'm a shy teenager once again, on my way up the steps into a library where a holy silence reigns as in a temple. Here the holy mysteries of scholarship are practised, in which I have to begin my initiation. I am filled with a sense of ceremony. Strange! I'd forgotten this feeling. Having no more spent my days in libraries than I had in national museums.

Norse Mythology. A yellow cover which rang a bell in spite of all the time that had gone by. Mysteries. Gunnlöth … Clashing-crags … the mead of poetry. Such pretty words, and each name had a number … whenever I heard a pretty word, it sparked off a number in my mind … Gunnlöth was seven … Clashing-crags, nine … and the mead of poetry … it couldn't be pinned down … nought, and another nought dripped from it, then a third, until the figure had turned into all figures and none of them, and was so big that it reached right round the world … everything and nothing this mysterious thing was which she guarded in a mountain at the land's highest point … heaven and earth above and all around in this realm of Gunnlöth's.

I shrug off these silly childish thoughts which actually I thought I'd forgotten, and ask the librarian for the *Eddas* and *Norse Mythology*. In Icelandic. Get hold of the whole lot. The book with the yellow cover included. Snorri's version is in there. I borrow the *Eddas* to take home rather than the book with the yellow cover. I find this yellow cover so annoying all of a sudden. And because it's just a retelling. I presume the librarian will think I'm an academic so that my cover won't be blown here as well. But of course he recognises the guilty teenager in me … no point deceiving yourself … it's the way I'm standing with the book in my hands. And all of a sudden I'm struck by something. Did I say guilty teenager? Yes, that's probably it. I wasn't a shy teenager. I was a guilty teenager.

I sat down with the book on the steps outside the Royal Library and looked everything up. On either side of me people were walking up and down the steps, my head level with their knees, and all I took in were these feet going up and down … up and down … up and down … I sat there a long time … for several centuries, surely, whilst the feet of the generations passed by, casting their flickering shadows over the pages as I read about Gunnlöth's betrayal … 'and lay with her for three nights and then she let him drink three draughts of the mead.' And there was I saying he'd stolen the mead from her! But then he left with it, of course … spewed it back up again … well, that's the sort of thing that's liable to happen in myths.

Sky and ocean and a mountain at the land's highest point! Unbelievably silly. Women never change. I got a bad taste in my mouth. But there was really no need for me to go getting worked up here on the steps! This land had sunk a long time ago. And I knew it. Remembered it on the toilet floor that time. That's why I'd lied to the lawyer and the psychiatrist and even to Anna. That's why I've never been able to bring myself to tell you about Dís's story. It's difficult to talk from the land of guilt, impossible almost. Because it's so deep down. The third land can get so heavy that it doesn't stay afloat. It sank down into the deep like Atlantis long before I remember, and no-one can get there without risking their life. And there are no telephone lines which go there, and even if you could hear my voice from there you wouldn't understand the language I was speaking. It's not a language of men. Because the land is populated solely by women and their voice is softer than silence. The odd woman nevertheless claims that it can still happen when the currents are right that the fish can make out the murmur of their speech in the gurgle of the deep.

And while I strode back home to Anna's with the books under my arm and everything which I remembered confirmed, my Dís is in this land of hers, preparing the mead … the mead of poetic invention …

The mead was a drink of goddesses and gods. It was so sacred that no-one was given it except those who served the goddess. And kings-to-be when they came to rule the realm, because they died twice. They died in the mysteries and rose afresh reborn, and were woken in a realm of gods and immortals with the holy mead. In the realm where glowing gold glistens like sun and like fire. Where cuckoos call and the ground grows with the leek's green growth and the ram sheds its fleece. Where each man who arrives is purged of sickness and age, and no-one can die. Where mead and meat never run short. Those who sip of this mead become god-like. It was made from earth and moon's excess and dedicated to the goddess of the sun. So that the sun shouldn't darken but rise afresh with a new year. And with a new king.

He who sipped this mead understood both things: the grand design and the smallest detail. Our sacred songs which the gods had taught us, about the nine worlds and what was there at the dawn of time opened up for him. His ears opened, a veil fell from his eyes. He comprehended everything and became of the gods. He acquired a language of gods and poets. Saw the connectedness of all things.

The songs of heaven and earth ring out like a single ode to life. The breast of the one who sips is a holy well of song worked from the life-song of all creation: of fishes and great whales in the ocean, and of all things living on earth and in air. Of the song of earth and harvest, of sky and rain. The earth of the king who ruled in harmony with this song would not perish.

The priestess gave a king-to-be the mead. In a hall more beautiful than the sun. It was in the enchantment of the mead in the beaker that my power over the king lay.

It was the legacy of women I had been entrusted with. The song of creation.

I'd often assisted my mother at the mead-making along with the other girls. Before I became priestess. I had gone to the beehive for honey. I had ladled the rainwater from the cask. I had milked the sacred goat. I had moved the millstones and ground the barley. And I had followed her up onto the heath and picked the meadwort. Now I remembered my uncertainty as I watched her on the heath. She was my mother – I was flesh of her flesh, bone of her bone – but her golden hair rising up against the sky and shining like a sun reminded me that she was another person besides. And that no-one possessed the whole of her the whole of the time. Not even I did. Her uncut hair reminded me that somewhere inside her were green grounds where not even I was allowed to set foot. Those holy shrines were hers alone. The village women who got married tied their hair up or cut their braids off as a sacrifice to the goddess Sif for fertility, placing them in wells, but my mother with her golden hair like rays of the sun upon her head was given not only to me but to the goddess herself, and was many different women. And so I didn't always know who my mother was. Was it my mother who danced on the heath and the goddess who stroked my cheek and helped me out of my shoes when they'd got wet with dew? Was it my mother who'd given birth to me or was it the goddess herself who was my mother? Was I flesh of Earth's flesh, bone of her bone?

Now I knew that my mothers were many. And yet only one.

Night-time. I'm sitting alone at a table in the pub at Anna's. Full of a sadness which Dís's tale has woken in me. And a hurt that can't be put into words. And the greater her innocence and the brighter her voice, the more saddening her beauty and joy. Unaware that her invention was a lament for me. This lament drowns out even the rock music coming from the side room which the teenagers haven't left yet, and for the first time in my life I wish for more noise. But the noise doesn't exist which could stifle this silent lament. Because I'm on the verge of exposing my daughter.

Anna had locked up. Everyone gone except for these leather-clad teenagers who she'd said could finish their game of pool in the side room. If they kept the noise down. Anna was taking empty and half-empty beer glasses from the table and stacking up dirty plates. Putting them on the trolley. I sat at a table over by the window where a ghostly street-lamp's glow blended with the faint light from the candle. There was a new stain on the red-checked table-cloth from the evening's drinking, and it stood out from the other stains. Not completely dry yet, but well on its way to making itself just as much at home on the table-cloth as the older stains.

Over on the edge of the table lay both the *Eddas*. Sæmundur and Snorri. I'd dragged these founding fathers of Icelandic culture into a dive in Copenhagen and now they sat there imposingly like judges on a stained, red-checked table-cloth.

I thrust Sæmundur and Snorri at Anna the next time she came near the table. But actually she was going flat out. And I'd got a headache. Couldn't stand this mixture of lament and rock music. Drums were being beaten inside my head as well. I had to yell for Anna to hear me. Having to yell like this got on my nerves, and flew in the face of everything I was used to. I'd always thought that convicted criminals were allowed to whisper their confessions. At least those criminals concerned with saving face.

It wasn't like that, I shouted.

What?

What I told you about Gunnlöth. It's not right to say that Odin stole the art of poetic invention off her. She … she …

Right, said Anna, stopping me in mid-flow, and said she was going to turn the cloth over, that it was cleaner on the other side, and while she was turning it over I had to sit with Sæmundur and Snorri in my lap and wait until she'd got this over with. I didn't think the cloth the least bit cleaner on the other side but as if I needed to wash my name clean after a telling-off I said:

I seemed to recall it. And I've lied about this to the lawyer and the psychiatrist and …

Hardly high treason.

No, but …

So who was she then?

And now there was nothing for it but to confess. No, not confess. Anna wasn't a judge.

She was clearly no goddess, I said, sensing the contempt creeping into my voice. She was the daughter of a giant and lived inside the rocks and the whole lot of them were demons and troll-women.

Right, Anna called from over by the trolley this time, at no point batting an eyelid. You'd be forgiven for thinking that demons and troll-women were regulars of hers. But she came and sat down with me all the same.

So it's all just rubbish then?

No, I answered hesitantly. Some of it fits. She gives him the mead to drink and sleeps with him.

Not bad at all. Go on.

He did steal the mead, but not from her. The mead of poetry belonged to her father Suttungur and he set Gunnlöth to guard over it in a place called Clashing-crags. And he didn't want to give Odin the drink. But she … hang on a second … it's in two different books, *Hávamál* and Snorri's *Edda*.

I got hold of *Hávamál*.

It says here:

Gunnlöth gave me
on a golden chair
a drink of the dear-won mead.

See, she's bringing him the mead there anyway. Or else I don't understand *Hávamál* well enough. It's an ancient poem. Snorri's easier to understand. Look, here's the version I learned. And Snorri says: 'Evilworker' – that's an alias, a name Odin went by – 'Evilworker went to where Gunnlöth was and lay with her for three nights and then she let him drink three draughts of the mead.' So you see that …

Anna nodded.

She let herself be seduced by Odin.

Yes, and that's how he got hold of the mead and made off with it, I said, feeling drained all of a sudden. Thinking to myself that any worries I'd had that Anna wouldn't understand were obviously unfounded. She got straight to the heart of the matter as she always did. As if she's always had demons and troll-women around her and spoken the language of giants' daughters. Seen the gills moving herself.

Same old story, said Anna.

Yes, I said, shamefaced.

Doesn't that spy programme on TV talk about getting information out of the girl in bed? I don't know … I don't get it. I never let anyone into my bed who thinks they're going to find my mouth between my legs. Here it is, under my nose. But then neither can I say that divine beings have made a big thing of trying it on with me.

And she laughed her husky tobacco-laugh when she saw that I'd become bright red in the face and tongue-tied. And it was not without a hint of irony in her voice that she said:

Maybe I've never been in love enough.

Then I sprang up from my chair and practically hissed at her: In love! As if that made any difference! Nobody betrays …

I bit my lip as if I'd been about to let slip something inappropriate. I can honestly say this sudden outburst of mine took me by surprise, but Anna didn't bat an eyelid.

And you were going to cover up for her.

Cover up? Yes, but not to begin with. It came about inadvertently somehow. I could swear. I just seemed to recall that Odin had stolen it. But then … yes, then I shut up.

So what about Dís, then? What's she thinking? – asked Anna, as if she were in no doubt that Dís was normal.

Thinking? Who can say?

And ask myself if that was the ending to this story which I feared most of all and was meaning to avoid when I wanted Dís to be only half crazy … or completely? Had she yet to commit the betrayal? Or was she covering something up?

Anna went on taking away the grimy glasses with smeared lipstick and dried beer foam on their rims and acted as if she saw neither me nor the founding fathers of Icelandic culture. I was still in a state after my confessions and knew I'd made a blunder when I reacted so severely to what Anna had said about love, but I was startled from my reflections when she suddenly opened the door into the side-room and called in to the boys with an ominous authority to be on their way and they obeyed with no objections and I didn't turn round but could sense their presence behind me: the rustle of leather clothes, the clomp of boots and the gravelly goodbyes which they flung at us and I knew that they'd won. Like gloating hunters, they stood bragging over their game. Sensed my helplessness.

I told Anna that it didn't look like I would be able to stop myself tracking down Óli. Although exchanging words with a person who had absolutely nothing between their ears was obviously pointless, it would at least put my conscience at rest.

I was pained and ashamed at giving in to Óli like this and I went on to justify myself, impatient, hard in tone, saying something along the lines of it being at the very least irresponsible not to try to question Óli about that fateful day when Dís wandered into the museum and saw she had time to spare, as she put it. So she must have looked at her watch, mustn't she? For the last time before fake time, as she called it, ran its course? But time to spare for what?

I thought Anna ought to understand how demeaning it was for me, having to turn to Óli for an answer, to this ... to this pathetic lad who I'd never wished to know anything about, of whom nothing would ever come, and who certainly hadn't the makings of a husband for Dís. But Anna smirked – she was above these emotions of mine – and wrinkled her nose up because Anna can smell the stench of misanthropy. To be sure, stronger than the rank smell of beer and more pungent than the reek coming from the simmering sausage pot is the stench of misanthropy in Anna's nostrils.

I got up in a sort of rage. Utterly defeated. Snatched Sæmundur and Snorri from the table and said that the cloths were no cleaner on the other side. Said I'd take them the very next evening to a laundrette which I'd seen was close by, and as if this were the most natural thing in the world, Anna said: All right. That she could do without the table-cloths in the meantime. That the tables were just as dirty as the cloths anyhow, so that no-one would notice even if they were missing.

All night long the sky god's voice was thundering in the storm.
The dogs growled and barked savagely. Caught scent of the
odour of men in the downpour and in the raging gusts of wind,
and in the flashes of lightning and angry hammer-blows they
sensed the god's warning. The trees howled and screamed,
their heavy tops swayed and their branches bent and buckled
and tangled together like in a furious whirling dance. The
tenderest stalks pressed themselves to the breast of mother
earth, terrified. No-one will sleep tonight, I thought, got out of
bed and sat down at the altar in my lodge. But I didn't pick up
on the storm's omen before the screeching neigh cut through
the noise of the wind and rain and an awful squall shook and
pounded the air. This neigh came from far up on the heath.
Where the herd roamed free. The herd was so far from the
village that not even on windless days did sight or sound of it
reach us. Only one horse had that kind of voice. The sacrificial
horse which the gods had chosen and announced through
a casting of lots. On the open heath it had run and roamed
about with the herd, awaiting its fate. And now its crazed voice
screeched out over the sound of the thundering storm. A neigh
like that could only mean that the one had arrived who would
attempt to capture him, cast the flying halter about his neck
and tie him to the ash tree. In this wild and fiery horse resided
the god who had picked himself out for sacrifice at the king's
consecration. If the king-to-be managed to defeat him. Single-

117

combat to the death.

All of creation was bringing us the news that Odin had arrived. Baugi my uncle had ferried him across the rushing river. No-one travelled with Baugi free from risk.

As the horse's neigh faded away I wrapped my robe about me and rushed out into the storm. No matter how ominous the voice of the gods is, a priestess is to have a part in it and not to spare herself. The darkness, crying out and moaning, had set every monster loose. The rain poured over me and beat against my face. I heard a crashing coming from Urthur's lodge and when I hurried over there I saw that the door was open and flapping in the gale, but Urthur herself wasn't inside. I carried on up past the women's lodges, felt my way along the walls until they came to an end and an unsheltered stretch began, the rain blinded me, bursts of wind sometimes lifting my robe up off my shoulders so that it stood out behind me like the wings of a bird, sometimes wrapping it around me so that I felt as if the spirits of Hel were twining themselves about me and letting me go again only to close about me once more until I became drenched through and carried the heavy robe like a second skin on my shoulders. The neighing above the raging storm drove me onwards. At last I was drawing near the boundary. I flung myself down on the furthest stone and stretched my vision to its uttermost, higher and upwards until I saw where Urthur was standing on the rock with the sacred carvings. Swathed in her dark fur she stood motionless, awesomely powerful and mysterious as if the ancient mother herself had risen up out of the night with her age-old magic and with a power above the gods themselves, for when she raised an arm to the sky the storm died down in that instant as if she had calmed the winds and air herself, almost dead-calm in the fading grey of morning. Then she turned in all cardinal directions and moved her lips and the chant slithered over like the wet mist which I knew she was conjuring up over this holy shrine. We were invisible to the uninitiated and our peaceful abode was like drizzly mountains to the eye.

Then the mist was directed at Odin. Until he had been led

to the mysteries and defeated the forces of destruction, he wasn't allowed anywhere except in the company of those who were initiated and enabled. And he was not allowed to set eyes upon the priestess until he was worthy of standing face to face with her, in the hall more beautiful than the sun.

Don't forget that you're a priestess.

I impressed this on myself. It never left my mind that I was to consecrate a king who it had been prophesied would be honoured beyond all kings. It was my duty to the nation and to the members of my family that the goddess and all the gods should view the king with approval. I had to ensure that nothing made them angry. That the king was steeped in the spirit of the rule so that he would be a wise and just ruler and keep peace and ensure the bounty of the earth and sea. So that the prophecy came to pass. My responsibility was a great one.

Dís had begun to speak with authority. There was a new tone in her voice, with more authority, yes, and more confidence. She spoke almost like an official, which of course she was. That's what they were, isn't it, these priestesses?

The powers of all of us were in tune. It was all a matter of waiting. Getting ready. The air was heavy with my father's voice as he taught the king-to-be ancient deeds of gods and men under the ash tree by the spring.

I'd so often listened to my father reciting at sacrifices that the chant sounded in my head as I went about my tasks … countless winters before earth was made … where earth came from, and high heavens … where moon and sun came from … and our lineages … and the law of our nation … sacred knowledge which the river spirits kept safe in the rocks and imparted to sacrificial priest and mighty sage … my father's head was filled with the speech of goddesses and gods, but the greatest knowledge, that which is hidden in sacred runes, is whispered secretly into the ears of the chosen, because the runes are of godly origin and harmful among men.

The mead-making was my responsibility. In the mead was nothing but the first foods of gods and men. Each task was the goddess's task when she made the mead for the first time at the dawn of the world. It now fell to me to perform all deeds of the goddess. As my mother had done before me. Now I was to grind the first ear of grain. Now I was to fetch the first honeycomb from the bee-hive and to ladle the first ladleful from the rain cask. Now I was to milk the first drop of milk.

I walked in my mother's footsteps although she herself was gone. But she was never gone from my thoughts. At times it was as if I sensed her presence as a shimmering glow and I took it as an omen that I was on the right path.

I held my hand out to her, spoke to her ... Dís love ... Dís my darling, but she neither heard nor saw me. Who had conjured up such a mist over me that I was invisible to her? Who? To what end?

Soon I'd go to meet with the god to pick the first meadwort.

I was so possessed by my work that my mind was perfectly focused, and it seemed as if Urthur was pleased with me. I could feel her watching over me, though she went about it discreetly. She followed the progress of the rites I conducted. She watched over my every movement. She never said I was impatient as she'd sometimes done before, or found fault with me. The moments we spent together were peaceful, and when I scooped the water over the ash tree in the evenings with her, I felt as if life would never change. No, I wasn't impatient, but felt that everything I got done had a purpose which remained for me to see. No uncertainty. I drank of Urthur's wisdom like a thirsty woman gulps down cool spring-water ... she'd taught me ... and taught my mother ... and though her warning to me still sounded loudly in my mind, it was a comfort that she'd said I was ready. Urthur was solid as a rock. As if she sensed I'd understood it was no use asking about my destiny or about things which still had to come to pass. That an oracle was only a clue as to the will of the gods. Not a way for mortal men to shirk their destiny. Urthur never says: you shan't … you shouldn't … you mustn't … That sort of thing is for weak-willed people who, by dabbling in sorcery and wicked spells, try to take the place of the gods and twist the rule to their own advantage, she says.

I sat silently in the prison cell. But now I started. Could Dís be correct when she said that Urthur had not once in the course of this long story said: you shouldn't … you mustn't … ? Wasn't she just getting at me? The old paranoia sprang up in my mind. Was she getting at me safe in the knowledge that this story wasn't written down? I couldn't look it up … this was an oral narrative … obviously anyone can alter things in it as the fancy takes them … put their own mark on it and send it out far and wide.

But it was because I wanted what was best for you … because I care about you. The magic circle, Dís. I didn't forbid you to do things except when you strayed off the straight and narrow. I wanted to help you … to make sure you learned something sensible so that you could get along in life, maybe take over the company … marry a husband you could rely on … it's not such a minor point, Dís, having a husband you can rely on …

… and she frowned as if my voice were a croaking bank of fog which was about to obscure a holy tree. Whispered:

I drove care from my heart … had faith in Urthur.

Then I went a little crazy. At her mention of Urthur. Indifference towards me. I was in a mist, reciting my runes in a fog which was filling up my brain … there was no way for me to shut up … I just wanted to make sure you could get along in life without incident … and marry a decent man. And that you'd be happy in life … be happy … my voice had become hoarse with fog … I heard a faint trace of this chanting as if it were coming from a tape-recorder underneath a pillow, and I had ceased to understand it myself. It was actually boring me to death. I wasn't the one who'd composed it, and I no longer had control over it, either. The recitation had taken control of me and moved my lips ceaselessly, like a machine I didn't know how to stop … it wasn't even my own voice any more … it was the sound of many voices … of different ages … some so deep and low that it was as if they were coming back from over the centuries … a plethora of voices which were all belting out the same thing … some of them I knew … yours … you were in this group of voices who were speaking through me … I'd become like an old witch, speaking in tongues. Finally I realised that Dís's expression was so troubled that her thoughts stood as if inscribed in fiery letters on the wall of the cell, made to put heart into her so that she should be able to endure this nightmare: Don't forget that you're a priestess, and Urthur wrapped her wide pelt around her to hide her from me. Then at last I heard my own voice:

I only wanted to shelter you from pain. I couldn't bear seeing you suffer.

I got no response. One of them might have said something. Urthur should have understood me. She knows what Dís has in store for her. What's so praiseworthy about keeping quiet and looking on without lifting a finger as she goes to meet such a cruel destiny? Why not stop her before she commits the betrayal, warn her? – I think, having arrived at the laundrette, annoyed at everyone. Tear the table-cloths one after another from a scrunched-up plastic bag. Chuck them in the machine. Every single one of them smelling foul, and they look more than anything like a red-checked dung heap when they're all together. To have to go and track down Óli now. When even Dís has stopped talking about him. Dump an entire packet of washing powder into the machine. Just as well if they choke in foam, bloody table cloths. They're going crazy in there with an angry growling red-checked noise, turn after turn tangled up in brawls, get free from the scrum and merge together again. Foaming at the mouth. I don't know whether they'll get out of this in one piece or in tatters which I'll never be able to untangle again. Broken-hearted over Óli! The foam spurts out of the soap-hole. And there's nowhere to sit except on this hard bench up against the drier with its handle in my back like a dagger whenever I go to lean back, at my feet the scrunched-up carrier bag which I carried here crammed full with filthy red-checked table-cloths from a bar. I sit there in a laundrette like any other old woman. As if I've never owned a washing machine, drier and utility room, in a detached house, all of my very own. As if I've never owned anything and never been anything. I'm one of the masses and I no longer have a name. In my mind, the thoughts pile on top of each other. Is Anna aware what a sacrifice this is on my part? It's just as if they take it for granted, these women, who can't tell apart sacrifice and everyday chores. Or Urthur. She could prevent everything, change it all. She could wave her magic wand over me and turn me back into the princess in the golden slippers in a utility room of her very own and release me from this instrument of torture which growls and grumbles, bubbling at the mouth like a fish and now I go suddenly crazy inside … everything is wrenched around inside me and my anger at Dís hurls all sense from me because it's her fault, that cretinous conversation in the pub, in which I, the civilised and rational human being, am drawn into an incomprehensible myth, an invention from out of some deranged prehistoric mind, and discuss it – with perfect sobriety! – as if this Gunnlöth were a fellow lodger I shared a utility room with, a person made of flesh and blood, as if she were a reality, and then this Urthur, this sanctimonious hood-woman who's claimed Dís – my daughter – as her own and who's smacking the life-breath out of me, slaps spells on me, makes me invisible, conjures up a fog over me, and where's Dís, then, while I'm groping my way along in this demeaning, unheard-of reality? Yes, in a wonderful mood – in a radiant mood – now happy and cheerful with Loki, now all sparkly-eyed over a king-to-be. She's not afraid of *them*. Not at all: she's afraid of nothing but herself. That she won't live up to her part. I'm trembling with anger. I'm beside myself with rage. The world swims red before my eyes …

I come back to myself when the water for the rinse trickles into the machine. It flows fresh and clear with a brook's refreshing babble and my mind clears. At which point I know that this load of washing isn't some sacrifice made for Anna's sake, but some sort of atonement or peace-offering – towards whom, you might ask, and I'm asking myself the same thing. I don't know, but Anna does, the one who was kind enough to let me rip all the cloths off her tables, even though she had no others to cover them up with.

I've got Óli's address. I remember when Dís slapped it down on the table before she left for Copenhagen. At the time I thought she was trying to provoke me. Chucking her address in Copenhagen at us even though we'd forbidden her from going. Pure provocation. It simply enraged me that she hid nothing from us. Because not much of what she said or did was to our liking. Because it was then up to us to conceal what she did, keep her hidden from others. We adopted this tone of voice. If you listen out carefully now, you'll hear it as well as I do. It's the tone which progressive, modern, understanding parents assume when they're talking about their teenagers with other people: a bantering crossed with a grim humour which convinces you and others that your children don't need to be taken seriously. You play down their strayings, depict them in a slightly comic light if they get out: these teenagers – turn your hair grey – it can be put right easily enough with hair-dye when they're back on the straight and narrow. We stick it out with a touch of bravado, having a laugh or two at the expense of the kid who's floundering along on the rough terrain off the edge of the straight and narrow path. As long as he remains within sight, at least.

Yet I put off tracking down Óli as long as I could. I had enough on my hands with Dís. And what could be easier to justify than allowing yourself to be detained by the supreme god. Choosing him over one wretched lad who'd come as far from the stock of his nation's kings and heroes as it was possible to get. There's one Icelander I shed no tears for, I said to myself, but he preyed on my mind. He was constantly on my mind. Now, when Dís seemed at last to have forgotten him, I was the one lugging him into the prison. Without anyone being able to see him. Couldn't shake him off. It was just as if I was carrying him as a mother carries an unborn child. A weight which no-one could feel but me.

She tells me that Loki is to collect the regal spear from the forge.

One morning she woke up at the crack of dawn and got up even though it wasn't yet time for being up and about. She didn't know what woke her. The air was calm but the turning tide of light and dark's grey glow lay over everything. Everyone sleeps at that time because turning tides can be treacherous. Things can always go either way. So it's best to turn to the ash tree, green in winter, so that everyone knows you go in peace. I walked up the path alongside the women's houses, going softly so as not to disturb the sleep of others. As soon as I came into the clearing, I saw that someone was sitting up against the tree-trunk. Loki! Long before I saw his fair hair shining in the hour's dim glow I was aware of him and felt it obvious that he should be sitting there. He had woken me, of course! He'd sent a message to me in my sleep. He was waiting for me. And yet it was just as if he had been oblivious to it, for he didn't look like he was expecting anyone. He sat calmly like someone sits when he's by himself. One of his elbows was propped on his knee, his hand under his chin. Staring straight ahead in thought. It was such a relief to see him after how serious and focused things had been lately! My spirits leaped and I snapped into a game, crept up on him from behind and put my hands over his eyes. Expected him to twist away, roll himself up like a ball of wool and roll like that down the hillside, me following like a second ball of wool. This was one of our old childhood games. But he seized my hands tightly and turned around sharply as if I'd taken him by surprise. His mind far away. So he had drawn me here unwittingly, then, as I suspected. And although I was overjoyed that the bonds between us were so close, I nevertheless asked him downcast if it might be that he hadn't wished me to come. I wanted always to be on Loki's mind. I wanted him to think about nothing else but me. But Loki quickly became his usual self. The smile in his eyes which could banish the gloomiest fog beamed out at me and drove off the mist of the hour. I sat down beside him under the boughs of the ash tree which never let its leaves fall and the spring was clear and calm at our feet. We sat silently for a while until he told me that he was on his way to the forge to collect the regal spear which I was to hallow and give to Odin at the consecration.

I fell silent. So my father must be in poor health, then. Never had anyone other than he gone to the forge. Such a great and uncanny holiness emanated from the smiths' craft that no-one went there except those who know how to guard against the magic of these wily workers. They were masters of fire beyond other men. They had an understanding of this force's magical strength. Charged their handiwork with the mystery of creation when they smelted with the crucible and hammered on the anvil. That's why the smiths had the goddess's anger forever hanging over them and were skilled in many spells for their own protection. Each item forged had to be an offering to the goddess. Each task performed was done to placate her. The forge was a long way outside our compound.

So Loki had sought this place out to ready himself for the journey. For next to my father, no-one had powers as great as Loki's. And knew how to turn spiteful words in such a way that the blights blasted the one who spoke them rather than him. I asked Loki to come back home unharmed but he said that he didn't fear for himself. That the smiths here weren't as powerful as the ones Odin had been describing. He'd been among nations which worked iron.

And now Gunnlöth's voice dropped and she began to

whisper like when you're terrified that something evil and taboo might be set in motion just at the mention of it. Her voice conveyed a dread to me which settled over the cell and crept into the bare stone walls enclosing us. I felt as if we were locked inside a rock. And the air grew thick with this voice which all of a sudden sounded familiar, like an echo from another world. This voice conveyed both dismay and terror when she said she'd sought out Loki's embrace under the ash tree.

Loki held his arms tightly about me as he'd always done when I was little and scared of something, but now I was a priestess, maid of the goddess, and my mind more receptive to her will, both her good will and her ill will and I knew that the working of metals was more dangerous than anything else because the earth has her own time and no-one can understand the sowing and reaping in her dark depths, and if her belly is cut, her rhythm disturbed, blood drips from the sun, moon and stars. When metal and stones are ripped from her insides her suffering cannot be described ... when she's torn apart ... wounded within.

Iron though! The word alone sends a shudder through all the worlds.

I hardly dared to say the word in my head for fear of the goddess's anger. I knew there were nations which were makers of a metal they called iron. They tore stones prematurely out of the guts of the earth and heated them in fiery ovens as if they were a mother's belly ... disturbed the rule of creation ... disgraced the goddess who sent us her iron down from the sky. We knew that her vengeance was horrific ... she was frenzied in her agony and fury ... she rose against those who did this in her most awful form ... every creature siding with her ... until men went wild ... broke oaths, and brother battled brother ... This metal was unearthly, and so mixed with evil that it was shut away at sacrifices in the village. It could never be allowed to enter the shrine of the goddess.

My vision dimmed at talk of this so that Loki's bright complexion seemed to pale and a shudder seemed to pass through the tree ... I could see that Loki felt it as well and I pressed myself more tightly against him.

Yet Loki went on talking about it ... from the boldness of one acquainted with the forces of heaven and earth, I thought at first, but when he explained to me that Odin had examined the marshes down in the village and said that it was possible to extract iron from them, he lowered his voice so that I could hardly hear him, until he fell suddenly silent as if his voice had faltered. I was taken aback. Never had I seen Loki in the grip of such despair.

I had to try to put his mind at rest. And though I was myself full of dismay over what Loki had told me about the marshes, I told him that no such danger threatened. No king would do such a thing without the knowledge of the goddess and the sacrificial priest. Our power was higher than the will of any king, he knew that. And as long as we were living and breathing, no-one would disgrace the goddess or her sacred residence in the fen-halls. As long as it didn't leave my mind that I was a priestess, there was no danger. Urthur's voice in my breast. And I made this certainty of mine known to Loki. And I added:

No king is going to forfeit his sovereignty by going against our will and the goddess's.

And when I heard her tone of voice – so sure of victory – jangling in my ears, it occurred to me that it was in just this sort of voice that the power to break things lay.

But Odin had put forward rational arguments which Loki related to her: he had said that the trade routes were closing because of the unrest of a people he called Celts and so it might come about that they couldn't get hold of gold or other goods, but if iron was extracted here at home it would bring us great wealth and we could forge weapons and tools ourselves ...

I took hold of both of Loki's hands.

Have you forgotten the prophecy? That Odin's name will be honoured beyond all kings? Such a king will never turn out to be a worker of evil for us.

No, said Loki, but sometimes ...

Sometimes what? – I asked, and at that moment my love

for Loki was no longer purely the love of a child but the love of a woman when she gains insight into the hidden worlds of her loved-one's mind. I perceived previously unknown regions which he'd kept hidden to protect the child in me. He went on with his account, breathless but his voice confiding:

Sometimes he speaks as though he fears nothing and puts faith only in the strength of his own two hands. He has such a way with words. It all flows. Fire smoulders in his eyes as though he's yearning for it. He makes use of fear ... he doesn't fear it ... sometimes I get scared ... scared ... and yet ...

And yet what?

He also says a lot about his travels among unknown nations. About banquets with kings. About contests and entertainments. Attacks and tight spots, too. A world unknown to me.

For an instant he looked at me and a prayer spoke to me out of the blue depths of his eyes. I was filled with sadness because I then understood what had previously been hidden from me. The pain that went with his ability. Although his spirit knew no bounds any more than the spirits of the gods do, his journeys through worlds were nonetheless the journeys of a lone traveller. Because he was far away even when he was close by. As though asleep and yet waking. Whole but divided. And he saw things the opposite way to other people. Asleep he was visible. Waking, invisible. Loki bore the mark of the goddess. I knew that he sometimes thought about the life led by others his age. They learned to wield weapons and hunt game. Had a rowdy time of it, holding drinking bouts and contests. Yet never had I heard him wish for such a life himself.

The peace which he'd talked about at the beginning had vanished. In his eyes, shadows and light were vying like twinkling rays darting out between clouds, but it wasn't the steady joy which I knew ... this joy was wild and erratic ... as if it enthralled him against his will ... he was struggling with it ... pressing it back. It blazed like sudden sparks in his eyes. And I understood that these sparks were a pale shadow of the fierceness which Odin carried within him.

The consecration will bring such fearlessness to heel, Loki, you know that. And then it could also be that this is valour, and valour is the mark of a king.

I know, Gunnlöth.

I stroked his cheek and asked the goddess to lend my fingertips the sound of the harp so that Loki might feel once again the harmony of existence and remember that in their loneliness, fear and suffering turn finally to their opposite in search of peace. Towards joy. I wanted to see Loki happy once more. He who'd always been of comfort to me in difficult times, had made me happy, had given in to my whims. Now I wanted to give him strength.

He grew calm but his eyes weren't capable of concealing the conflicting emotions within him. At that moment I understood Loki's weak spot. It was the transparent blue veil of his eyes which let through every feeling, every hurt. A play of colours which was easy to read. They were open and unguarded. I'd sensed this as a child and made use of it. My power over Loki had been absolute. So what about others, whose intentions were not pure? What if the terror of the forge proved to be more than he could stand? If forces stronger than those he commanded gained a hold over him? Then I said:

Loki, never let your enemies look you in the eye.

And in a flash Loki made light of our conversation as he usually did. He leaped to his feet, so high that he almost got his mane of long fair hair tangled in the ash's leaves. He shook himself and said laughing:

Dealing with those worms at the forge is going to be fun.

The candle's burning out on the table where I'm sitting in the pub. The flame's grown weak and wavering above a cone of old hardened wax. Inside this cone of wax there's a candle-stick holder which can't be seen. Anna's not one to bother with cleaning the wax off. It just drips down, hardens, and heaps up bit by bit around the holder. The flame rises out of this mountain of wax like a column of fire out of old lava. It often seems like the light is going out for good but then it flames up once more and castes a feeble glow over the dead wax. I can't make my mind up, like the candle.

I shuddered at the thought of going to look for Óli. Felt now as if it had been a rash decision to make, and that an obsession had had the upper hand. But I've grown superstitious. I feel as if this decision to look for him has become almost a fateful pledge there in the laundrette. As if I'm obliged to stand by it if I don't want something dreadful to happen. It's not natural, his face appearing in the wax whenever the flame of the candle flares up. A face set into the dead matter in this forge. Waiting to break free.

Him, break free! – I thought in a fit of anger, snuffed out the candle and stood up so violently that I almost knocked the chair over.

I'm the one who needs to break free! I've had him on my back long enough … wandering along to the prison with me … staring at me out of the candle …

Anna had just locked up after the last customer and was tidying up. I told her that it would be best if I got a move on with this Óli business.

And Anna said:

It's best if the Fish goes with you.

I was speechless. No end to the blows that come my way. A silent prayer to Anna started off in my mind which I repeated over and over again:

Anna, oh dear Anna, don't put me through this. Not him … I've somehow got such an aversion to that man …

Finally I said out loud, attempting a bit of bravado to convince her:

I don't need anyone to come with me. I know where he lives. Dís handed over the address. She seems to have been living there when it happened.

You need someone to guide you, said Anna.

That's how she put it. As if I were about to go down to the underworld. I had no choice but to give in without further resistance. And understood that a person who's on their way to an underworld of drugs doesn't get to pick their travelling companions. Still less do they deserve an escort of angels.

If I were depicting us walking in a film, I'd film us from behind. You're never more undefended against other people than when you turn your back on them. You're seen, but without seeing yourself. I sometimes think that all a person's suffering is captured in this vulnerable rear view. Show me how vulnerable you are and I'll put down my spear. Have to watch out that I don't put it in my own flesh. This is how I felt later when I stood behind the policeman. And watched his wide black unwavering back come to life.

Besides, there would be little use in showing you my face because I'm hanging my head and not looking anyone in the eye. Precisely this can be seen by looking at me from behind. In my sinking shoulders. I can't hear the Fish at my side except when we turn a corner. He's wearing flat, open shoes with soft soles and when we turn a corner he steers me in the right direction by slapping the sole of his shoe down flat on the pavement. The sound makes me think of a fish's tail being smacked against a rock. That's how I stay with him without glancing up. Look him in the eye no more than I do anyone else. Just sense his presence. His instinct shows me the way on this stooped walk where the sun and stars are nowhere in sight, and the flow of people now carries us forwards and now breaks over us, and the Fish wriggles clear of hidden skerries and navigates me up out of whirlpools. I don't really understand why we got off the bus so early. Judging by the smell and people's movements, these are just ordinary people in an ordinary part of town. The underworld must still be a long way off.

The Fish had laid down three rules to guide me. To have a banknote to hand which I can get out in a hurry and hold out to a mugger or a beggar. To have my eyes about me without staring like a tourist, and number three, to leave him in charge of our journey. And then he added that I obviously didn't need to be afraid of anything in broad daylight. That this wasn't New York.

Defiance welled up in me at this last comment of his, purely because it was him, even though he'd said it to reassure me, and I was on the verge of saying haughtily that Dís would never have sunk as low as the low-life in New York! He understood how I'd reacted even though I said nothing, looked at me wetly, his calm pupils swimming in water like drops in an ocean, and I understood then that it's no use putting on a show in the face of the elements and knew that it was only a matter of chance that I wasn't following Dís's trail in an underworld worse than this one. This was an underworld, no matter whether it was called Copenhagen, New York or Reykjavík. Reykjavík? I'd never gone out to look for her in Reykjavík. There was no underworld there. Or was there? I ought to know if there was. Is there? Ought I to know? Didn't want to. Now everything that I didn't know – all blissful ignorance, all heedlessness – had turned to pain. But I had to get a grip of myself. Continue to swim with the Fish. Not sink. The tail slaps.

We turn a corner. I look up. I'm startled. I'm confronted with dark-skinned men. I get scared. I once ended up on the wrong street in Harlem. I was coming out of the Indian museum and took a wrong turn. An endless row of black men was hanging around against the walls as if they were propping the concrete houses up on their shoulders. A black earthworm stretching the length of this row of houses, along which a menacing silence crept in time with my appearance. There's nothing more dangerous than being a traveller in an underworld. I suppose you really need to weave your own fame in words to escape with your life. I felt as if I'd stepped in an instant onto a different continent. True enough, here they're standing not in lines but in clusters on the pavement; some of them are sitting on chairs outside the shops. Women in silk trousers or saris walk up and down the streets with babies. This is an immigrant quarter. So alien that I remind myself that I'm not allowed to stare like a tourist, but still I keep my eyes about me. The Fish's advice not actually necessary because I can feel that fear and wariness are stamped in my passport. The eyes of the men outside the shops follow us. With my head down, I dart my eyes in that direction and think I can make out a trace of insolence in their look, as if they were letting me know that it was thanks to their mercy and clemency that I was visible. They know that I am despised. Or else I wouldn't be here. But I grew calmer at seeing women and children, and there on the corner was a greengrocer's. Apples, oranges and a round green fruit unfamiliar to me. And nuts. Lots of different kinds of almonds and nuts. A strange mixture of the familiar and the alien about this grocery shop, as with the area as a whole. And yet I was filled with a sense of security. It was just as if someone was leading a normal existence. As if I viewed these things as protection. As if Hell would be easier to bear if there were women, children and fruit there. And that in some way justified my visit there. Made my errand less shameful. And I wondered whether anyone would win me from this Hel with their tears … no, what nonsense, this isn't an underworld … Óli can't be here for we swim onwards, and I can't get Óli off my mind. Or Óli's parents. Our acquaintances at one time, and acquaintances of our acquaintances before that. There was no disagreement when they were accepted into the New Year's Eve club, being our kind of people with a taste for evening dress and caviar; yes, they were people of such good taste that they vanished from the club of their own accord without kicking up a fuss when their difficulties with Óli could no longer be concealed. Spared our feelings so that we were able to miss them free of guilt and say, as we were wishing one another a happy New Year, what a shame it was they hadn't been able to make it. Now we're next in line, my friend. I'm afraid that we'll be obliged to have prior engagements next New Year's Eve.

And of course, the immigrant quarter was only a waiting room. A kind of transit lounge. Because now the fish-tail slaps again. We turn a corner, crossing yet another boundary and I know now that we've arrived. I don't need to be told. First it's the noise. Rock music beats against me like blows. Then the litter which the breeze sweeps together into a grey eddy on the corner, and the dust which gets in my nose and throat and all over me. All at once I'm wrapped in a veil of grey dust. People aren't clustered together here. Here and there a lone human being sits on a pavement or stands up against the wall of a building. And even if two or more are seen together, it's still just as if each one is in perfect isolation. The houses hang about, dreary and dilapidated. There's a doomed look about them and the breathing from their passageways is intermittent. I try not to look. Try to keep up with the Fish who's swimming on at the same pace and with the same rhythm and instils confidence in me. He steers me into one of the passageways.

I brought myself up close to his side. In spite of my aversion, I felt that he was my protector. I acknowledged it. Due to the fact that ... don't we sometimes say that someone is in their element, like a fish in water? I can't find a better way to put it. But I was glad you couldn't see me. I was glad you weren't there. Óli's mother, on the other hand, was just as close to me as my own ghost. I don't know when she joined us, but she walks by my side like a spirit. I don't dare look over that way.

Inside, in the middle of the passageway lay a heap of old household junk, a rusty cooker, a torn sofa with the springs exposed. Abandoned remains of human habitation in Hell. In this quiet, dreary passageway we sensed something moving suddenly right by the railings. I stopped in my tracks because the sight hit me like a blow under the ribs. A young girl sat like a hump in the ground with a baby at her scrawny bare breast. The child rested perfectly still in her arms, its eyes closed, and seemed to be sleeping without letting go of the nipple, sucking feebly every now and then as if it were drawing more sleep into itself. The girl didn't move despite us turning up. She made no sound. Watched us blankly out from under a matted tangle of hair. It had at some stage been blonde. Silent, calm like an image of the Madonna in a church. The magic circle.

I pulled at the Fish's sleeve.

We have to do something, I whispered.

He looked at me expectantly as if he were waiting for *me* to make a decision.

But *I* didn't have a ready answer and the Fish set off again as I admitted that I was at a loss. I was filled with resentment. How was I to know what should be done? I didn't know my way around here. And the Fish refused to take the responsibility off my shoulders. He walked on and I had no choice but to follow. Right by the door, a rat shot out from under the steps. I thought for a second that I was going to faint. The Fish glanced over his shoulder to see how I was bearing up but neither of us said a word. We went on up the creaking stairs without speaking. The place reeked. The Fish knocked at a door on the second floor. We could hear signs of life and at one point I could see something move through a chink in the door. A while passed before the door was opened. A young man stood in the doorway. He looked us up and down without saying anything and didn't ask us in. I said I was looking for Óli. He answered me in Icelandic.

Óli doesn't live here any more.

Where does he live?

He shrugged to show that he didn't know. Or didn't want to say.

I'm Dís's mother, I said, in the hope that he might give me some clue.

I don't know anything about Dís. I've already told the police that. She'd already gone. Took her bag and said she was off. Gone, like I've said already.

I was taken aback. It hadn't occurred to me that the police would have come here too.

Were the police looking for Óli?

They were looking for everyone and everything. But I don't

know anything about Dís. She'd already left. I don't know what she's doing, bringing the police here. I'll end up having to move as well.

Don't you know anything about Óli?

He shrugged again, exaggerating all his movements as if to show his contempt and indifference.

Obviously found himself another guardian angel.

A guardian angel?

A girl.

There was such utter contempt in his voice when he spoke this word that it was just as if he'd got a taste in his mouth of the rat we'd come across in the hallway. I straightened my back and went on resolutely:

But you said Dís was already gone. Is that right?

He nodded. The Fish stood beside me without saying a word. But he filled the corridor. I could feel it and no doubt the boy could feel it too. And now I turned to the Fish, my guide through this abyss, in the hope that the currents might be turning now and that he'd be able to make out the burble of my language and be able to tell me whether I'd understood correctly that Dís had hidden a clue here like in a treasure hunt. But fishes don't speak. They slap their tails and as I was no longer an unwilling member of the shoal, we walked down the steps side by side. Abandoned the place.

It might of course be argued that I'd put off tracking down Óli for too long. The boy could naturally be lying about the whole thing to cover up for Óli and to make out as if Dís had been acting alone and that Óli had never been involved. And Óli, of course, had fled. No way of telling whether he knew anything about a terrorist group. Or could help take the suspicion off Dís. In that respect, my journey here served no purpose.

But it had now become clear to me that this wasn't the reason I'd tracked down Óli at all. I was looking for something else. And although I perhaps never found what I was looking for, I meant to follow the magical ball of twine.

Things had become clear in my mind. I decided to take the Madonna in the passageway home with me to Anna's. Home to Anna's. But when we got downstairs, the passageway was empty. The Madonna had left.

Have you ever needed to nip out down to the underworld? I'm only asking, now. Because there's really so little we know about each other. I don't even know whether you know your way around the back alleys of Reykjavík any better than I do. It's mainly when Laugavegur is pedestrianised in the run-up to Christmas that we've been forced to pick our way along side streets. When our Mercedes is banished from the main shopping street and we get this yearly shock just before Christmas. And we've always tried to strut along on foot, puffed up and dignified and a little bad-tempered past all these people who had sprung up all of a sudden to tread on one's toes in the crowds like rats scurrying out of their holes.

I'm tired, I can tell you. Tired in my body. I'm so tired that it's just as if I've been hard at it lugging coal. Or salting fish. I can't keep my head up.

The Fish knew what state I was in. He made sure I got a seat on the bus. Stood next to me the whole way. He didn't leave my side. He steered us straight into the pub. Anna was serving beer and sausages. The Fish had me walk inside ahead of him, and the doorway was packed tight with youths. And owing to the exhaustion, I paid no particular attention to the miracle until afterwards: the group of youths in the leather jackets parted before me like the Red Sea, and I walked in, my feet dry. Me and the Fish. The crests of waves on either side, skin-headed or dyed violet. Closed behind us and the Fish led me to his table.

Looking back on it, I feel as if he maybe sat me down on a chair, but I must have sat down by myself. Let myself drop. My knees like boulders which I couldn't keep aloft. Yet the Fish was on his way over to me with a mug of beer. Unasked for, naturally. Because here, it wasn't allowed to ask for anything. Demand anything. Have an expectation of anything. With longing, I watched the cool drink draw near and took a gulp of it, yes, swigged it down until the exhaustion grew numb and nerves slackened, sleep not far off when I got to my feet. I felt I'd sleep better tonight than I had done the thousand previous nights. I'd rid myself of a burden. The exploration which I'd put off for so long was over. I held out my hand to the Fish to say goodbye without speaking a word. Certain that he could hear what I left unsaid. He'd swum with me in the deep. Had heard my voice.

I went to my room and slept.

The night was drawing near when I was to go up onto the heath to pick the meadwort. On the last full moon of the harvest month it opened its flowers. No-one knew where this kind of herb bloomed in winter-time except us, and it was surrounded by great secrecy. Because the meadwort was to the mead what flint was to fire. The herb imparted a godly soul and fire to the drink. Bursting with magic-laden sap of the moon, the herb promised life and death and life once more … the eternal cycle … immortality.

I followed the moon's progress as it waxed. Slow and sinking in the sky, the gods' horn of plenty was filling up. Everything was readying itself for creation. The goddess's energy needed to flow in my blood. I fasted the final three nights and drank only pure rainwater because I wasn't allowed to drink water which had already made the earth fertile. And on the night when the full moon was shining and brimming over with excess sap, I went up onto the heath.

I moved with such a strange ease. And although dressed only in a white kirtle, I didn't feel the cold. My hair loose and unadorned. My mind was also at ease and I was unafraid, because the chant of the women at the millstones sounded in my ears as they ground the barley which was to go into the mead, the chant to ensure peace and bounty which decreed that nobody should harm others, work evil or cause death, and further off as an accompaniment to the Lay of Grotti, Urthur's chant sounded with its mystical rhythm as she addressed the moon so that neither spite nor withering words should harm me this night.

I walked through the forest on my way up onto the heath. The slope wasn't steep and the forest's soft undergrowth was like velvet underfoot. The forest started thinning out the further up I got, and the moonlight was of ever more use. The moon's rays fell down like silver rain between the branches of the trees. Then it was as if I walked shining pools between scattered trees and finally I'd got out onto the moon's ocean, when the whole heath bathed itself in the all-embracing brightness. On this night no living thing was sleeping. Every little flower was awake in its red and yellow bed of heather. The little birds which sprang up twittering and darted in between tussocks settled back down again at once as if ashamed of having momentarily forgotten themselves. Sheep stopped in their rumination, snorted. Further up on the heath the horses, their chests puffed out and heads held erect. Everything was waiting as I was for the moon's precious sap to brim over and bestow its surplus upon us.

I sat down on a tussock. Everything was calm. I listened to a stone talking to a flower and a flower babbling to a bird. The breeze carried to me everything whispered in lovers' ears all worlds over. I waited for the marvel to happen, for the moon god himself to descend and invite me to sip of the drink of life. And just then, he shone like silver and gold. Swollen with life, wild with generosity … now he was letting the sap brim over … and I stood up and opened my arms wide … and let my robe fall … the meadwort opened up and the energy filled my whole being, I danced naked … and the heath in motion … the girls had come, their bodies a-quiver to the air's song, and its notes carried me ever higher and higher … the trembling dew-drops cupped inside flowers, the moonlight flowed … coursed with my blood, my body's rhythm in harmony with the earth where the roots of the meadwort trembled expectantly for the waters which flowed to earth with a surplus of life and enfolded her and everything floated in the water, earth, moon and stars like fish in the depths of the sky, and I like the horn of plenty itself ... like the goddess ... so full to the brim ... my chest bursting ... my loins burning with life ... I couldn't stem its flow ... nothing in me could be stopped ... it was from me that life flowed ... I had to give ... this was what I had to give and I stooped down and picked the first meadwort. So luminously bright. Dressed in the moon's hue and scented with the moon's energy. And the air was filled with a neigh from the horse ... wild with impatience ...

In that moment I sensed something moving unexpectedly by the trees on the hillside below me, as if a shadow were wandering there. What was that? A creature? A person? Something I'd conjured up thoughtlessly and without meaning to? A furtive shadow. A spirit roaming, gone astray? Loki? It couldn't be Loki. Loki could never conceal himself from me with that fair hair of his. Loki could never become a fleeting shadow in the dark. And it would never have crossed Loki's mind to violate the sacred night of the goddess. This shadow didn't stand out from the darkness. Only by moving had it been framed for an instant in the darkness and taken shape. Then it was gone. Disappeared behind a tree. Who had come here onto the heath on this night? Had he seen me? I didn't hear anything. But he couldn't have seen me. The mist was concealing me. And no-one was capable of seeing me while their eyes were held. No-one able to see before being permitted to sip of the draught of life and the veil fell from his eyes. Before he'd entered the hall more beautiful than the sun and made it through the clashing crags before they slammed together. I could make out nothing else. The breeze had fallen silent.

I picked up my robe and wrapped it around my naked body. I must have been seeing things. It must have been a branch moving, or a fox. Or an apparition wandering while its spirit slept ... straying off course in the mist of the heath?

I walked down from the heath with the meadwort in the palm of my hand. The girls stayed behind to pick what was needed to fill the bowls. For a moment I thought to warn them.

But I didn't. I let the moment of hesitation pass until it closed behind me like the clashing crags themselves.

Urthur was there to meet me when I got home to my lodge. She spread the pelt over me herself when I lay down to rest. I was drained to the point of exhaustion and I didn't know whether it was dreaming or waking that I saw her sit by my bedside long into the night. Until everything became dark and silent.

Urthur and I were ladling the white water over the sacred tree.

Urthur was taking her time. She was standing by the trunk of the tree and I felt her presence strongly as I knelt at the spring and sank my hands in the white mud at its edge. I was taking my time as well. I wanted to enjoy feeling the mud run softly through my fingers like a healing ointment before I filled my palms with water. I felt a gentleness coming from Urthur which wrapped around me and filled me with calm but I was also troubled by a heavy heart because autumn was seeking refuge in the water which reflected the dwindling, faint white moon's approaching death. No longer a bright mirror for the sun, as in mid-summer.

I rose and sprinkled water on the trunk. And while my palms were still resting on the trunk, Urthur asked, her voice soft and warm as if cloth had brushed against my ears:

Are you ready to swear the ring-oath, my child?

My hands grew still. The ring-oath of the priestess. Before a priestess served the precious mead she was shown the object which was holiest of all objects. The golden beaker which was kept in the hall of the goddess. She was allowed to set eyes on neither the hall nor the beaker nor lay hands on the beaker before a ring-oath had been sworn. It was the highest ring-oath a priestess swore. From that point on, my devotion to the goddess came before everything else. All my training had had this end in sight. The bark of the tree of which I usually had no feeling in my fingers became rough under my palm as if a barrier had appeared between me and the ash. Hesitation hindered my fusion with all creation. Urthur waited as if she had been prepared for this. She altered neither bearing nor manner but the tone of her voice was more everyday when she went on speaking. The warmth hadn't gone, and yet her tone was more like the one she used when she was discussing the task we had at hand. I knew that she was bringing out in me this hair-fine balance of head and heart which she said was proper in a priestess.

She said that Odin would soon be led to the mysteries. That my father praised his diligence and thirst for knowledge and had now granted him the guidance which would serve him on his journey to Niflheimur and the nine worlds as well as teaching him those precepts which a righteous king would have to follow.

Has Loki come back with the regal spear?

A natural question for a priestess to ask, but it came too readily. Urthur pretended not to know I was on tenterhooks for an answer.

Yes, she replied.

My joy that Loki's journey to the forge had come off was mixed with disappointment and surprise. I had been expecting Loki to come to me and relieve me of the anxiety I'd been under on his account. He was supposed to take me in his arms and boast of his boldness and accomplishment. He was supposed to come and allow me to rejoice with him over his talent which prevailed over the sorcery of the forge fire and warded off the mighty spells of the smiths. Why didn't he come? Even though my mind had sent him messages ceaselessly …

The smell of autumn was strong in my nostrils. And everything in sight heralded winter in a way which hardly seemed natural to me. The thoughts of the trees already seemed bowed to the earth, their branches drooped, letting ever more of their colourful foliage fall to the ground. The rowan trees' red berries had become food for birds fleeing winter. Swans flew overhead in the moon's pallid glow; bold in song they obeyed a call from the kingdom of the dead. Everything sank in the same direction. There was no-one about by my father's house … no Loki on his way to me … no bright notes were brought to me on the air … a heavy unspeaking wind picked up and brushed the tree-tops around the sacred glades which appeared like islands in the fields … I turned my eyes towards the glade nearest to me where the trees stood guard about the marsh of the goddess and all of a sudden I saw … the shadow was still abroad. The trees shuddered. They were trembling like I was. What was it? An omen? The shadow of winter? Or a black raven struck suddenly blind …?

I could feel Urthur watching me. But she remained silent. She could detect my heaviness of heart even though I'd said nothing. Her question remained unanswered.

I looked at the vanishing moon. The first night of winter is drawing near. Moon is losing his might. His abundance of life ebbing away. The forces of death hounding him. It's the swift sky-wolf who's running behind him. Ravenous he snaps, jaws stretched wide. The wolf will soon devour him. Pitch darkness throughout all the worlds.

Will a new winter moon be kindled? Will a world rise afresh?

A neigh from up on the heath made its way into the silence of my thoughts. The horse was still running free, wiry and tensed, the heath marked by his hooves, but now I could picture him as he stops suddenly in mid-gallop, rears up and tosses his mane, the swish of his mane falls silent, his lip curls back exposing his teeth, his eyes are crazed as if he too has seen a shadow. The autumn wind which chills my thoughts makes its way to his nose and his nostrils quiver. He catches scent of his destiny. Sees the halter in the hand of the shadow who has come visiting him. Lifts his head, and the neigh bursts from his throat as if this voice is tearing him apart with its divine power, as the craziness of one who knows his death is near at hand mingles with the pride of one chosen by the god. Beneath my feet the earth trembled because such sounds from a son's throat pierce her heart like a spear, and tinged with blood are the tears that trickle from her eyes.

The whole world was reminding me of my role.

It was my role to win the god from Hel with my tears.

It was my role to charge the moon with enchantment for battle with the wolf.

I mustn't fail a king-to-be. I had to give him the goddess's vital energy. He had to live through death, so that everything might live.

And my eyes sought out the burial chamber. The evergreen ash spread its boughs out above my head, but Urthur had taught me that beneath the earth's surface, one of its roots stretched its way into the chamber, a root which was both trunk and boughs and was the measure of worlds. That all things were reversed in Hel's dwelling. And Hel's dwelling is at the same time the womb of mother earth. That's why the man will be led there in order to obtain wisdom of all worlds. At once dead and unborn. I was reminded in this way of the eternal cycle of life and death. And I knew that I would have to dispel the shadows which were breaking loose in my mind, intensified by Gunnlöth's longing. By short-sightedness and impatience, as Urthur sometimes said.

Don't forget that you're a priestess.

Urthur had left without my being aware, without asking for an answer to her question. Her patience was as eternity, although her eternity is a moment for me. She imparts the wisdom of all generations, and at this moment I thought back over the teaching she'd given me. Ladled water from that well:

Moon, by which we reckon the years, dies but rises new again. He is reborn in death like this so that time can begin afresh and order come upon the world. Moon's death is a sacrifice to ensure the eternal onward course of life, so that night might follow day, summer follow winter and new year follow old. That is how it has been since the gods created full-moon and new-moon. It is the lot of a king who creates a new realm to live the moon's destiny. A new realm begins. A new time in the life of a nation. It is a king's lot to sacrifice himself to death in order to be reborn. New. Other than he was, and yet himself. That is what the first sacrificial king did when the world was re-created the first time. And that is what all kings have done since. In the sacrificial rite, a king obtains the wisdom of the gods and the mighty runes' secret in order that the world might be formed afresh, and that the new time might bring us bounty and justice.

But between new and old, everything is unformed. Forces of destruction break free from the bonds of time. Wolf devours moon. Should the wolf not release his prey, the end of the gods will come and a world will perish. So moon must be reborn in order that the eternal cycle of life and death might endure. In the burial chamber of the first sacrificial king, a king lives death. He fasts in order to cleanse himself of life lived previously. He will be pierced with a spear so that he might feel the horse's destiny. Rivers will come to his aid. They preserve the secrets of the ancient runes. And your father conjures up life-force in the burial chamber. His head like a shrivelled bag containing age-old wisdom about how the sky and earth were formed, and the ancient deeds of gods and men. Sings a mighty song in each world. And all things, living and dead, must win him from Hel with their tears. But the king himself will have to seize the great runes of the mighty god. If he seizes them his enchantment will have become such that he will be able to undo the bindings which tie us to the short-sightedness of time and space which never persists for more than one lifetime at once, and he will understand that he is still living. The one who travels the nine worlds beneath Niflheimur has thus died twice and so the king will achieve immortality like the gods. And be allowed to sip from the draught of immortality which the goddess alone has control over. He has lived through death and so shall everything else. Such is the rule of the goddess.

In the darkness of this autumn evening as I lay unsleeping in my bed, the door opened silently and Urthur entered. She sat down on a seat and I knew that she had come to me for my answer.

Urthur sat silent for a long time and my breathing grew gradually steady and rose and fell in harmony with Urthur's until finally there seemed to be but a single person breathing. Then I got down onto the floor and knelt at her lap. She put her hand on my head and asked again:

Are you ready to swear the ring-oath to the goddess, my child?

I am.

When I came out of the prison I seemed to feel autumn in the air, and I thought I saw an autumn moon above me in the grey-white glare. It's just as if I'm vanishing into Dís's invention.

I was seized by a peculiar urge to see the moon.

I tried to stay sensible. Told myself that Gunnlöth's reality wasn't my reality. Tried to be rational. Stared up into the sky and assured myself that I wasn't out by the light of the moon but under a feeble spring sun. It was the spring sun that was shining. April already having arrived. I knew all about the moon, what's more. I'd seen it on television. But my feet carried me onwards. Past the tall iron fence where the dog sniffed out a greeting at me. Past Anna's even, even though I carried her mark on my shoulder, and on I walked … I seem to recall getting on a bus … although that might have been some other time, but at last I'd arrived at the hospital garden. I remember sitting there on the bench under the oak tree. I sat there for a good while and when evening drew on, clouds started banking up in the sky and a wind got up. The moon didn't make an appearance. I had to make do with coaxing forth the moon which I had stored away in my mind: the grey, dry and desolate ground where a man's trying to get a footing in zero-gravity … the space-suit holding his umbilical cord to earth like a caul about him … it was just a con, of course … no-one really knew space without severing the umbilical cord … without whirling around crazily in the void … the man was jerked back … he was snatched

155

back here at the exact moment when he'd never seen a more glorious sight than of the earth from out there, where we were sitting in our armchairs and watching him on television. If it weren't televised we would see nothing. I know that there are a great many foreign bodies up there among the sun and moon and stars. I can't see them with my naked eye, these globes of earthly origin, but I started to mull over whether I would be able to feel that they were there anyway even though I didn't know of them, and never watched television, say, or read the papers – in short, even though I didn't keep up to date – would there nevertheless live in me a fear of the spaceship's earthly driver … or of some sort of wolf or serpentarius? Some sort of suspicion that they could shape my destiny?

The stage had now been reached where she would be allowed to set eyes upon the golden beaker in the holiest shrine of the goddess.

She spoke haltingly, her words filled with a fear-tinged reverence: This is the holiest shrine of the goddess … from the dawn of time … which our rivers raised to her in ancient times from stones so large that the gods themselves must have carried them half way. The hall of the goddess is made from these sacred stones, walls and ceiling alike, and roofed with a covering of earth so that from the outside it is like a mound to the eye … the grass which grows upon the dwelling of the goddess may never be cut, and snow never settles there … it is green all year round where it stands on the hillside below the life tree … no-one dares to desecrate the dwelling of the goddess or make much noise close by it, and no-one is allowed there without swearing her a ring-oath, for it is here that she manifests herself …

This description of the landscape seemed familiar to me, fresh in my mind. And it suddenly came back to me that Dís had described this to me before. At the outset. When she came out of the tunnel with Gunnlöth and Urthur.

But Dís, isn't this the mound, this green one, right by the ash tree … don't you remember … this one which was still green … ?

The words stuck in my throat. It suddenly pained me to have

157

to remind her of the dreary landscape which she'd described at the outset, a scorched wasteland, withered grass, a sun way off course. When she put her faith in the eternal cycle. Why should I sap her strength with the truth … she was walking to meet her destiny … not until much later did I remember that she'd come back from this journey even though she herself seemed to have no better recollection of it than of an event long since passed, from a life lived previously. At this moment I was like Urthur herself, knowing past and future in the same instant, and yet hurrying after the magical ball of twine as if hope of being able to catch her up lay dormant in me.

A slight tremor passed through her slender body when she continued. This moment was so enraptured that I felt as if even the walls of the prison were listening in.

When I had bathed myself clean, Urthur led me to the altar of the goddess at the holy tree. On the ring I swore loyalty to the goddess and made an oath to preserve all that was hers: country and kingdom so that peace and prosperity and justice should rule. A pact between me and the goddess was made. If I kept faith with her, the good fortune she bestowed would always be with me.

A tunnel led to the hall of the goddess. That's where we went. A stone lay at either end of the tunnel, bars fixed to each. Out-stone and in-stone. Clashing crags which locked about one unworthy of being there and enclosed him in this dark passageway. He who sat shut in between them was neither alive nor dead. You had to know a chant for the bars to open up. Now I learned it off Urthur. And I walked into the narrow tunnel on towards the most sacred mystery of the goddess, into the living flesh of mother earth, and those beasts which are most sacred to the goddess guarded my way. They were carved onto the stones, snakes and horses coloured red, as well as the suns of the goddess and the axes of the sky god, and we were enfolded in a warm and gentle gloom like beasts from ancient times, and I seemed to sense water trickling somewhere …

And I'm still pondering the riddle. I can see a glint of light in this labyrinth. I seem to know where I am. Been here before …

heard it being described, I mean of course, but right now I don't know whether I'm leading Dís or she's leading me:

This must be the same tunnel, Dís, which you came out of at the start ... when you ... when Gunnlöth led you out.

Dís went on as if in a trance.

This time I was to go no further than the tunnel. And only look into the hall of the goddess. But as soon as the in-stone opened, a sight was revealed to me so marvellous that I fell to my knees on the stone threshold. There on an altar stood the beaker.

The beaker gave off such brightness that it was like a sparkling lake to behold and the brightness flowed from its source and out into the passageway, over me and through me like a golden river. I was at once both its channel and a pebble on its bottom. I was bathed in gold. Here was the source of the mysteries. A joy went through me which quenched a thirst I didn't know had afflicted me and sated a hunger which I didn't know I'd been gripped by, and the joy was made from air and water, earth and fire, and swelled in my chest like song ... an uncontrollable confusion of song which rose and fell like a bubbling hot spring simmering over the earth's fire until it grew steady and took shape, enclosed by the lip of the spring, and finally became a clear liquid in a golden beaker that trembles in a man's hands without a single drop going to waste, and when the golden joy dazzles my eyes and the brightness doesn't disappear even though they close and the sight gets inside, then you understand, you finally understand, that you yourself are made out of gold. And now I also understood why no-one who had seen the beaker was equal to the task of describing it for others.

In the transparent blue of her eyes I saw into the wide open expanses of worlds and remembered what she herself had said to Loki:

Never let your enemies look you in the eyes.

When I think back on it she's like a sun at that moment in just the same way that she appears to me now as a waterfall where she sits between the two guards in the row of seats across the plane from me. A sun in blue jeans and a baggy blue shirt which hides small breasts and delicate arms and a superhuman strength which is meant to bring a man/horse/moon back to life when he emerges from Niflheimur. And for a split second, I'm granted vision from outside and over the earth. It's as if I'm flying out of this prison cell into the immeasurable distance of the depths of the skies beyond every last written word, and I can see no fault committed by her. A sun like that can commit no betrayal. Yes, I think it's … stronger than everything that's strong, she sits there in her lodge face to face with her destiny. The giver of life herself. Submits to it. Doesn't forget that she's a priestess. Takes the regal spear from the altar. The priestess's role is now to inscribe the goddess's sacred signs on the socket of the spear for the king's life and good fortune.

Now both have the same destiny. On this night, eight nights before the holiest night of the year, I shut myself away to meet with the goddess in my lodge, and he was led into the burial chamber. The secret path which led there passed below our grounds and I could make them out from some way off before I shut myself away. Like shadowy underworld creatures they passed by in the night's pale light on their way to the sacred burial place with the man. My father was leading, the horned helm upon his head. Following him … a slender man, fair, beautiful … yes, it was Loki! Loki had demonstrated such great powers that my father had entrusted him with warding off those evils which will be greatest here in the world when the bars of Hel fall … I watched him for a long time as he drew away from me. Then came my father's men with cornets and horns and drums, and finally the king-to-be, the uninitiated one whom the grave-guard stopped. No-one gets inside unless he gives the goddess a ring, because mighty is the tree on which he must be borne before the mysteries open up to him. For his own well-being he handed the guard the ring which is meant to soften the mood of the goddess who rules in Hel. Although I couldn't see the ring, I knew how it should be. My mother had once told me that such rings looked like coiled snakes of gold, for from the top-most circle there dripped eight others, one ring for each night, nine rings and yet only one. And when the ring was given, the womb of mother earth opened up to receive the man. No man could get in through that opening upright. The man flattens himself. Wrapped in snake-skin. Is imbued with the nature of the creature which lives on despite shedding its skin. Slithers into the earth down a long and narrow passage. Earth and stones and darkness fill his mouth and nostrils until the bars of Hel open up. A hall coiled with serpents' spines, which are carved onto all the stones. And every stone charged with the spirits of ancient rivers which reside in them. The air as close-knit as Urthur's weaving. The black caw of ravens. Moon's grabber howls and pulls on his chains. The snake-man wriggles his way. At the centre is an ash-root which has become an upright gauge-tree which is the measure of all worlds. The snake-man winds his way up it … is seized … hangs tied from the tree of life which holds up the firmament … has become the centre of the universe …

A table was set up in my lodge. On it stood a beaker with water from the holy well for me to sip, but no other nourishment was allowed to pass my lips, neither solid nor liquid. I lit a fire. Sat down with the spear. The silent flames lit up my lodge and cast a flickering glow on the walls. The constant play of light and shadow surrounded me and the spear had taken on the colour of the fire. It glowed in my hands. And I admired the skilful hand of the smiths. Black from fire and soot, knowing the bowels of the earth as well as worms, they had worked their ode to the goddess in gold and crafted an object so beautiful that it was as if the gods themselves had lent them their hands. The serpent coiled about the socket of the spear, its horse's head raised. I took hold of the stylus and inscribed signs of sun and cycle on the socket of the spear and charged them with those songs which I teach no-one, neither lad nor married man. I sipped the water of life. The songs of the goddess cleared a path for themselves, the songs which in ancient times created sky and ocean and earth. Out of a murmur where all tones – mellow and mordant alike – combined in a single sound. The goddess's enchantment moved my tongue and finger, and my mind became far-reaching as the world's wisdom as I hallowed the spear and prayed to the goddess to protect king's life and limb. I charged my chant with sorcery to the point where it was chanting itself and cast a spell, decreeing that the one who owned this spear would be ever victorious under attack.

My strength was failing when I finished the chant. The world was spinning as the world of the man in the mysteries was spinning. Both of us were beset by hunger and thirst. I took hold of the spear and walked out into the night. It gleamed like a sunbeam in the dark. I heard the thud of the loom and walked straight to Urthur, bringing her the spear. She could feel the spear's and nature's sorcery pulsating in her hands and knew that I'd succeeded in my task. She looked into my eyes with an expression which I hadn't seen before but I knew that she sensed the proximity of the goddess as I did. Urthur didn't say a word, but in her manner I could feel her confidence in me for the approaching holy night when burial chambers open up and there is pitch-darkness throughout every world. When forces harmful among men roam free and join battle against the king-to-be, the man, Bestla's son ...

No, I wasn't supposed to think of Odin as a person, but rather as king-to-be. It was the rule of the goddess that a king-to-be was given to the goddess of Hel before the goddess of life and sun consecrated him. She had made that destiny for him herself and so was unable to release him from it. Sorrow over one's own actions the bitterest of all sorrows. Two goddesses, and yet one. The struggle within my own mind.

Don't forget that you're a priestess.

I had to be undivided. I'd sworn the goddess a ring-oath. Grief for the king-to-be fighting the forces of destruction would have to govern my actions. Now every thing, living and dead, had to be invoked to come to the man's aid. Win him from Hel with their tears.

And on the first night of the new year when all burial chambers opened up and dead men rose and came visiting the people in the village who put food out for them in the household shrine, I sat curled up in the dark corner of a prison and tried to impart to her all of my strength. So that she should rise unharmed after this night. I feared for her. Her eyes were smouldering. She was at once both close by and distant, by herself and yet everything around her seemed to be living. All is chaos. There's no measure of time. Nowhere a beginning or ending. The dapple-grey mare tramples the roads of the air frantic with grief over the fate of the horse who is spinning around the tree, of which none knows from what roots it rises. Jódís spurs the mare on. Its mane flutters like wings. A doomed man hears the baying of dogs, he looks over his shoulder and Jódís snatches him onto the mare's back with her ... eight feet tread the Hel-road. Everything is whirling. Sun doesn't know where she belongs. Most of the moon has vanished. The man is still hanging on the gauge-tree. Fire is blazing. Jaws are snapping. The steed snorts in its mortal struggle. Wolf and raven gorge themselves on the life of doomed men. Blood is dripping. The aged tree groans. Corpse-swallower rages ... and the night-black storm howled and whined upon the thatch of the roof as if it had something to settle with me, its tone deep as the first convulsions of the dead man who is called to out of the ground, and I was the one being spoken to. The storm had settled inside a man's throat. The man was calling out, invoking the goddess in his isolation as I had done in the forest facing the wolves until I understood that everyone has to experience their moment of suffering alone. That's why I remained silent. I knew what the man hadn't yet learned, that initiation into the ninth world eradicates fear. Overcoming your fear involves suffering. You have to grapple with it. Like with the wolves in the forest. Then you understand for the first time that it's not life and death which are opposed, but rather life and fear. Why should people fear the isolation of death? That loneliness lasts only the short moment before the clashing crags open and the wheel is whirling once more.

But then I made out a brighter tone than I expected in the heavy weave of the storm's noise, as if a delicate golden thread had been twisted into woollen cloth. The air filled with words. This wasn't the voice of the king-to-be. Why did he stay silent? Was it true, then, that he was afraid of nothing? What could be the reason that it was this bright tone which trembled? Why was it searching me out, as if he too were bound in fetters of darkness and earth? I recognised the voice.

I'm terrified.

Why are you terrified?

The goddess is attacking me. She wants me dead.

The goddess has many faces. Hel is Sun and Sun is Hel. Everything is on a whirling wheel…

Ask her to let me go. You're a priestess. You know what she wants.

No mortal woman knows for certain what the goddess wants.

The voice sounded most like it was coming out of the pitch-darkness of a wolf's gaping jaws. Why was Loki terrified of the night and death and the goddess? Loki, who knew the rule better than anyone else, Loki who had worshipped every tree and every leaf, learned songs off birds and off brooks' babbling and sung the praise of all creation? It was just as if this person speaking in the storm was terrified of everything but broad daylight.

Only you can give me light.

All my strength left me. Only the goddess was addressed in that way. Even in his distress, Loki should know that neither I nor the goddess was allowed to relieve him of his isolation. But Loki wasn't talking to the goddess like a man at a consecration who invokes the almighty mother. He spoke to Gunnlöth as if I possessed the power of the goddess and yet he surely knew that the rule of the priestess encloses my heart like a coat of mail and prohibits it from cracking, and the heart's agony then is more bitter than if it were allowed to crack into a thousand pieces, and the agony teaches this heart that love is cruellest to the one who nurses it in their breast. I wasn't allowed to coo back to the bright terrified voice like a mother to a child. That was something I had to save us both from. If Loki were tied to the goddess in her fearsome form, he couldn't choose to tie himself to her maternal form instead. He had to know the goddess in all her forms. Only in that way is it possible to rid yourself of fear of the goddess.

I'm not the goddess. I'm Gunnlöth.

And I stood up and my voice rose over the storm and over the murmur of weeping, dying creation:

Even when the goddess takes up residence in me, the whole of her is there. In her most baleful form as well. Or else I would be like a broken beaker.

A dead calm came on. Out into the void I whispered the only piece of advice I knew.

You have to call on the goddess yourself. She is in you just as much as she is in me.

And my tears fell heavy as gold. They were my offering to the goddess. A call for Hel to release what she had, but I wasn't allowed to ask for leniency. Or for her to give in. The one who needs to pass through the clashing crags of fear mustn't be stopped. He would be stuck in Niflheimur and not get back from there. The agony of isolation would be whirling in his head for ever more.

I sat silent in the prison cell. Saw that she'd also been speaking to me. I don't know whether she realised it herself but she was leaving me behind in my misery. She was washing her hands of my suffering. Leaving me behind, alone. The magic circle burst apart ... she was gone ... I was standing alone ... the opening menacing like a wolf's open jaws ... I had no strength ... the milk long since run dry ... nothing in my breasts except sleep ... I can't stand knowing that you're suffering, I'd always told her. That's the truth, but just now the agony of my own isolation was harder to bear. Yet another paradox of love, using others to shelter from your own suffering. It's hard to negotiate, this narrow ridge-path between love and cruelty.

And my arms have been left empty ... nothing to clutch on to ... myself like a child sucking on a dark empty hole, dark like an unseeing eye, pitch-dark as if the moon were inside a wolf's gaping jaws, and cornets are thundering in my ears. And the ninth Mighty Song. The beguiling gulf. The rune most charged with power awaits the man. The man head to heel with the world ... the roots of the ash tree in the sky ... the upright becomes reversed and the reversed upright and everything turns to its inverse ... the man no longer a man but rather every animal and plant ... he is the tree of life itself and senses how the tree hungers and thirsts ... parched ... the moon nowhere to be seen ... vanished into the void ... the man sees visions ... the moon and he have become one ... tries to get a footing but floats, lacking gravity ... un-made ... can see across the beguiling gulf... the earth herself pitches and tosses ... doesn't know where she belongs ... he feels she is floating ... burning ...

And in that instant the storm fell silent and silence alone reigned. Fires play about him. All the rainbow's colours in the flames ... he manages to ascend above the beguiling gulf, as if he were the newly-made moon itself ... the man's strength and power divine ... his own strength monstrous ... conjures the Potent God out of the gaping mouth of death ... the almighty prophet among gods rises ... the man stretches out his hand ... clasps it shut ... the rune of release in his hand ... his bonds fall away ... neither time nor space constrain him any more than they did the first god ... a new creation ... rebirth ... the man falls down. Free.

Everything was calm and quiet after the night's terrors. The forces of chaos and the beguiling gulf lay exhausted and defeated. Day, cautious like a callow young girl, eyes narrowed as if it hardly believed that the glow on the horizon heralded a new sun from the sea. A new year had been granted us.

I was standing outside in front of my lodge. There was not a sound to be heard. It was as if both beasts and men lay worn out after their struggles with ghosts and apparitions. Later on today the people in the village would hold a festival, eat and knock back no end of beer, and listen to wise women telling their future. Place rings and clay beakers in wells and lakes and marshes as a sacrifice to the goddess in the hope of peace and bounty. And although I was faint from fasting and staying awake, my mind still strayed to the feast which Loki and I had talked about before, where I would sit in the place of honour with the most beautiful gold-embroidered band about my forehead and the new king at my side, and I would hand over to him the spear which I had charged with spells to bring him good fortune and which Loki had collected from the forge and then I would see Loki again … Loki would make new songs for me … no, I had to get a move on. I had to make a sacrifice to the goddess at sunrise.

As I approached the shrine the calm was broken by the measured tramp of the horse to be sacrificed. Tied to the ash tree, he had endured a night of chaos. The halter marked out a place for him and it could be heard from the incessant hoof-falls that he was circling the ash tree, but the rhythm was broken every now and then by a sudden, impatient scraping, as if the memory of running free over the heath was struggling to get out against his will. Then he remembered his destiny, when the rope pulled taut. Continued his circular journey. Spun around the world. Then he became aware of me. Stopped and lifted a weary head. Snorted. Stood still, waiting. Could smell that I was near, knew that one was approaching who was bound by destiny no less than he was. He let me put my arms around his head, stroke his sweaty withers. I lifted the forelock from his eyes. They were calm and sad. Were animated momentarily with pain when he became aware of the life unexpectedly seeking a way out in shuddering jerks and twitches. He knew the thread of his destiny. Knew it would be cut. I learned then that twitches of life cause more pain to those with foreknowledge than life's ending. His lip quivered. I waited in case he thought to bring me a message from the gods with his voice, but he was silent. He had spent the night in nine worlds and seen the great mystery that can't be related. He is the sacrificial beast who brings us promise and affirmation of the eternal fusion of earth and high heaven, just as ice and fire had united in the beginning to create all the worlds. Just as everything sacrifices itself by fusing with its opposite to kindle new life from its death, this divine horse sacrifices itself. In death he is god and king.

All of a sudden this noble beast bent its head down to mine. We met for an instant in the middle of the clashing crags, one of us by the in-stone, the other by the out-stone, one bound for death, the other bound for life. I could see that suffering and fear had been left behind. The eyes still whole and undamaged, but the look in them far-off. In his loneliness he had already gone to meet the opposite in search of peace.

I made my sacrifice to the goddess and waited for evening.

Around the time when a new moon would rise in the sky, I was to serve the mead to the king-to-be who would be honoured beyond all kings.

Today I was allowed to break my fast. I was given vegetable broth to drink and bread, and I rested until the meal had fortified me.

Two girls went with me to a holy pool where I bathed. The living water closed about me and washed me clean. Its softness and energy and purity gave me strength. I felt as light as air. I felt I was soaring like the swans which swam here in summer, within me the wisdom of these wise birds who know earth and air and ocean.

The girls dressed me in a garment of white linen and I felt neither heat nor cold. From the pool I walked to the tunnel, past the holy ash tree. The horse didn't lift his head. Only his ears pricked up. He could hear as I could the men who were making their way from the burial chamber with the new king, the one who was stronger than he was. And I sensed that Urthur was close by. Although I hadn't seen Urthur for a long time, I knew that she had her eye on me. Her will was close by, directing me towards the tunnel. A moment when her image appeared in my mind was always the right one. Nowhere a void which fear and doubt could turn to their advantage.

I headed once more into the tunnel to the shrine of the goddess, behind me the two girls who were to help me adorn myself. My head swam from the strong smell of mother earth. Never before had she been so pungent in my nostrils, and I understood that it was the fasting which had cleansed my body of all impurity. It was as if I was no longer myself but part of mother earth. Her paths both above and below me. Her smell was the smell of my own flesh, the air that I breathed in was her spirit in the stones which lined the tunnel. The darkness wasn't the terror of the unknown but rather a lightlessness which was waiting to spark into life as its opposite: the great light at the end of the tunnel. This knowledge kindled my joy which flowed on ahead of me in the darkness like two golden brooks. And now I was allowed to step over the threshold into the brightness beyond words of the hall that was more beautiful than the sun.

There the king-to-be was to sip the precious mead.

Glowing gold cast such powerful rays onto the stones of the hall that the serpents with their raised horse-heads flickered in the glare, the edges of the sky-god's axe glittered and the sun-signs shone so dazzlingly that it was as though the air were filled with countless suns. When my eyes grew accustomed to this magnificence I could at last make out the object from which the brightness issued. In the middle of the hall was the golden chair.

Its arms and back decked with golden shields.

The golden serving-beaker with the precious mead on a table by its side and two drinking cups of pure gold. Their handles, the serpent-horse with its mane standing up on end.

Behind the throne the gold-decked bed had been prepared.

I was overwhelmed by such sanctity that I was struck motionless.

A small chest stood on the floor. Inside, my ceremonial attire, so bright and beautiful that I was dumbstruck. The girls picked up each item and silently helped me adorn myself. A belt of gold they fixed around my waist, around my arms golden rings which coiled like snakes up to my elbows, and about my neck they fastened the ring of the goddess which was fairest of all rings, set with red beads of amber. On my shoulders they placed the blue-black mantle with a scent like the violet in the meadow and they fastened it at my shoulder with a pin set with red agates. They combed my newly-washed hair. It fell free down onto my back, but about my forehead they fastened the gold-embroidered band. All of these jewels shone like glowing gold.

The garments and jewels of the goddess were laden with sorcery. My head swam from their holiness. It sapped my strength ... my head grew strangely light ... above and below me a cloudless blue sky as if I were a bird flying ... or a fish swimming in clear water ... all obstacles are lifted away and I am able to see through hills and woods. I am here and I am also in the sacrificial grove where my father is piercing the horse and the god's blood is dripping, flame-red, and a sacred ring is glowing on the plinth and casts beams of light on everyone there, my father, Odin, Urthur ... and Loki ... and my father reddens the plinth and the ring with the beast's blood ... sprinkles it on the king-to-be ... leads him to the plinth to swear the ring-oath ... and I am not only in air and water ... I am also in the sun's fire and all of us are one and the same act of creation ... we can hear the stones breathing and the trees growing ... the speech of birds is the speech of all of us because we are all things, live and dead, we are the same refrain in the single murmur of everything which lives and everything which dies and everything which lives and everything which dies and everything which ...

And I don't know whether I'm me or my father or Urthur or a rock or a fish in the deep or the very ash itself holding up the sky. Everything is an offering to the goddess in this moment. And I heard Odin's voice slither its way into this act of creation as he swore by sun and moon and the almighty goddess to abide by her rule.

There he swore to the goddess a ring-oath that couldn't be broken, guaranteeing peace and bounty for aged and unborn alike. The ring-oath floated in the air and wind. And there it will always float, whirling with the wheel of the ages, indelible ... the memory of it a piece of myself forever ... of all of us ...

part of my consciousness even though I stood now in the hall of the goddess once more ... had become myself and more than myself and yet less myself than before, and I think of the aged and unborn whose lives are staked on the luck and good fortune of a king. And I called upon the goddess that I might never fail her, that my powers might strengthen the young king who has risen from Niflhel to lead his nation. Just then a memory like the faint swoosh of eagle's wings awoke in my mind's clear blue sky. A childhood memory which the goddess sent to me at this moment, upon which I knew that Urthur's prophecy would soon be borne out. I would fasten eagle's wings on a young king to reward his courage and deeds and to mark his glory, that he would be allowed – like the king of birds, keen-eyed and free – to have his dwelling-place right by the gods and yet on earth among men, and soon he would be led here to me, and when the oath's great song died down and dissolved into its separate tones, my ears caught the faint measured strains of recitation which I sensed in eternity's harmony as a steady accompaniment to the least whisper and to the loudest thunder, but could only make it out for the first time now, when everything else grew silent ... it was Urthur reciting the prophecy of the king-to-be ... in the clotted blood and entrails of the horse she could see the threads of destiny in the woven fabric of all of us ... I could only hear that destiny as a vague chanting a vast distance from where I stood dressed in the attire of the goddess and I only sensed it dimly when the girls disappeared, silent and hanging their heads from fear at the moment's mystical holiness and it seemed to be at that moment that Urthur came rushing in. The prophecy's secret was still in her eyes and there was such an intensity about her that I didn't dare to speak to her, and before I knew it she had dashed over to the chest and snatched a strange-looking object from the bottom of it which I hadn't seen before. Such an immense brightness issued from it that even Urthur slowed in her movements. She held the object out to me but it was so dazzlingly bright that I didn't think I'd be capable of taking it. Then she told me that this object belonged solely to the priestess and ordered me to look into its shining surface.

It was a sun-disc with a handle, adorned with the circular signs of the goddess. Its handle was short and formed in three sections. Its lowest section was a ring; in the middle, an oval loop connected at the top to a bow-shaped loop which finally curved around the sun-disc like a frame. The disc itself was circular and its sparkling surface reminded me of the surface of the sacred well on a calm, moonlit night. There was harmony between the shape of the handle and the ornamentation on the disc. But on the disc the ring was open at the top like a beaker or bowl and the oval rings curled outwards from there to both sides like the orbits of eyes, and inside them were circles which were pupils. And suddenly I saw a face in this great sun-disc and so radiant were its eyes that I knew it was the goddess herself. The eyes grew ever deeper and deeper until I could see to the bottom. The goddess herself in the beaker. I stood face to face with her and the joy which shone in her eyes flowed through my whole body like blazing water … a hot joy which grew deeper and rose higher … it was swelling in waves inside my breast and now sought a way out in silent song. My mind filled with gratitude. Now I knew the goddess … I've looked in her eyes … seen the nation's goddess.

When I handed the object back to Urthur I realised that my manner had altered. The goddess's neck-ring made me stand tall. It formed a frame around the joy. The lips of a beaker restraining the shapeless seething of water boiling over a fire so that it didn't brim over. It was the snake which coiled itself around the earth and held her in place. I saw that Urthur had told me the truth. Here was the great peace, the bright joy so absolute and mysterious that no-one could enjoy it free of fear except the one who knows the wolves. This was the joy which was the opposite of fear. This is what Urthur had taught me. And I heard her voice in my blood: remember that only she who has tested out the mysteries on herself is fully acquainted with them. Urthur's wisdom like a well which never ran dry. If she had heeded my fear I wouldn't have known this joy which was at once bounded and boundless and which the goddess couldn't be without on this day, a joy which makes all suffering and all sacrifices endurable. A joy which blew fearlessness into the breast of another so that he should be able to approach the source of all life's mystery and become a channel for truth and justice himself. So that all of his actions should become like a song in praise of the goddess, mother of gods and men.

Urthur placed the object back in the chest. A decree of fate was burning in her eyes. I read her thoughts:

Don't forget that you're a priestess.

How can that be forgotten?

She who has looked into the eyes of the goddess must forever keep Urthur's words buried in her memory. I could feel that I was as the goddess was meant to be today: proud like a queen bee, her speech mild as honey but her mind sharp as a spear. Her power indisputable.

I held out my hand to Urthur. Everything she had taught me from the beginning was now in my body like blood which knew its course. We walked hand in hand up to the golden throne. I sat down on the seat of highest authority and I was hardly aware of Urthur withdrawing for just then it was as if the stones of the goddess's residence came tumbling down and opened before all the worlds' wide expanse so that I could see the world over. Had become the goddess, and as if the goddess had become a symbol of herself, I spun in all directions and in all times in a space which was boundless. And my ears made out a speechless astonishment. All of creation was holding its breath.

She was left by herself.

There was a door which faced south. It was in through this the king-to-be would come. It's right in her line of vision where she sits on the golden chair in the middle of the hall. And so she will be right in his line of vision, in her dark blue mantle, with her fair hair like a flood of sunbeams on a never-ending day in summer. Then I began to hear deep sounds as if the bellowing north wind was tearing itself free from a deep heavy sleep, a weighty message of rivers and ancestors in its voice. It was the procession drawing nearer and I knew that the procession was followed by more than an unperceptive eye could detect. I watched my father's hand as he opened the bars at the in-stone which opened for no-one except those who have learned that spell. Horned helm upon his head he opened it, full of might, and close behind him the musicians and masked gods followed, stepping lightly. Next the dancing girls in corded skirts with their breasts bare and rings of the goddess about their necks, and finally, last of all …

Odin is led into the mound.

He halted abruptly in the doorway. Flinched, his hand shooting up as if to shield his eyes, stepped back involuntarily. Having emerged out of a gloomy tunnel … out of Hel's pitch-darkness he seemed to be seeing a new earth rise up, bathed in golden rays. A fiery globe in a cloudless sky. Stock-still, aflame, he stared for a while until a quick, pained look of suffering passed over his exhausted face and I knew that it shot through his mind, yes, there was no doubt it shot into his mind that all this splendour was only an illusion, shown to him but not granted.

But the vision didn't fade from him. The sun with bright golden hair is watching him with two glittering eyes, life's liquid in a beaker by her side where she sits on the throne of heaven.

She watches him. And to begin with she thinks that he is an illusion too. For she seems to see Loki standing in the doorway. And just then she understands that Loki will never fade from her. No matter how many lives she is granted. Even though she is the sun itself. She stares at the man and can easily recognise the slender, wiry body, the high nose and the set of the mouth. She motions for him to come closer and understands then that her mistake stems from the fact that the gaze of the goddess is made from gold, gilding everything upon which she directs her vision. The men were similar, so much so that they might even be confused, and yet there was a world of difference between them. Odin's hair was dark auburn, not gilt with flame. Appears red because it has been reddened with the blood of the sacrificial beast. His beard, auburn. Dark, heavy brows, and his eyes set deep. And he's standing before her and she can see that he doesn't yet dare to trust what he sees. In his sad look she can still detect strains of the black flutter of ravens' wings coming from Niflheimur. It's uncertain whether he knows that one of his eyes won't come back. A globe-of-the-brow sacrificed for moon. She sees he is in need of life and healing.

The man is exhausted and bewildered and he drops to his knees before this wondrous vision. She directs her rays upon him. He is sworn to her by a ring-oath. The draught of immortality is his reward, hope of life and nourishment. She ladles the mead from the golden beaker and fills the cups with the serpentine handles. Holds the drink out to him. He stretches out both his hands as if a blind man were begging for sight and receives the cup. The cup trembles in his grasp. He

177

clenches his hand around the serpentine handle and waits for it to grow steady. She raises her cup and both of them raise the mead to their lips in the same instant.

Burning fire is unleashed through her body. She is blinded by this fire. She senses a power and a passion which take hold of her mind and body and grant the man life. Ladles out again. He gulps, thirsty, starved. Life moves into him ... new life ...

Meat from the sacrificial horse is brought in and set before them.

They eat and drink.

They are in the land of the undead where mead and meat never run short. The notes of the cornets sound as if from the depths of the earth, the horns address the sky and the bells on the drum tinkle as if water is playing on a brook's shallow bed. The dancing girls begin the dance. Like orbiting suns they dance around her and the man, to the glory of sky and sun, veils are flying, the cords billow around their loins like the stalks of wheat in a field, their sexes open and giving, blood courses through veins rhythmical and dark, and nothing measures the passing of immortality and infinity except this rhythmical, deep red arterial throb and I can no longer make out the words ... I don't even recognise the voice ... that isn't Dís's voice ... or Gunnlöth's ... hardly the goddess's either ... perhaps it's the sound of the rule itself which I hear when she stands up with the draught of immortality in her veins, breasts hard, and can feel the water blazing in her womb ... her body is burning ... she is earth and sun and water ... the goddess given over to her own rule that life should live ... she who knows the mysteries, at this moment she is the mystery itself ... suns burn in her eyes when she fixes her gaze on the man ... the girls remove the mantle from her, the gold-embroidered band, the jewels ... the goddess, naked, demands impregnation ... powerful and cruel and completely consumed by her unwavering demand for creation and re-creation, she won't stand for hesitation or backing down ... life must be what both of them long for ... his good luck and fortune depend on him bowing to her will when she invites him over to the bed decked with gold. Lays an arm over him in order that unsown acres might shoot up and butter might drip from every stalk …

I flew home. I've been struck by the lightning of the truth. A veil has been stripped from my eyes. I was light, weightless, freed from a spell, and filled my lungs with air as if I were coming up out of a deep, deep dive. I'd been holding my breath. Hadn't dared let a sound pass my lips. Not even when she sat down in the golden chair! I had to see Anna right away … kiss her, tell her the news. Gunnlöth didn't betray anyone! Dís had been right all along! She wasn't making any of it up. My feet carried me like wings!

I had the street to myself. No-one to hold me up. I was going so quickly that the dog behind the iron railings didn't even have a chance to greet me. And I played a prank on it. *Woof*, I cried at it as I hurried past. The cars were streaming by of course … they were streaming by exactly as they were the first time I came this way, to be sure. But now I felt they were giving way to me. Yes, that's how it felt. Because I was going flat out. Shot like a rocket. *I knew it … I knew it … I knew it* was going sing-song through my head to the beat of my winged feet on the way to Anna's …

I pushed the door open.

She didn't betray anyone!

I called this out across the room. Held my arms out to Anna who was standing behind the counter. Then looked triumphantly about me. Not many people there. One in the corner over there. Another in the opposite corner. Not regulars, and they looked at me with surprise. Didn't matter. My trinity were sitting together at a table, the Fish and the little woman with the head-scarf and the girl with the red curved lips drawn out onto her cheeks. Anna had stopped short in the middle of tipping sausages into the pot and stood deadly still with her tongs in the air as if posing for a photograph, stared at me astonished and – quite out of character – lost for words. Until she got going again and regained the power of speech.

It's really something to see you smiling!

Smiling! I was over the moon with joy!

I hurried round behind the counter, took these ridiculous tongs off her and spun her round. Laughing, she broke free:

Are you trying to tip the sausages over, woman? What's happened exactly?

I pushed her away from the counter and stretched up to the shelves for glasses.

Now I'm going to treat you to a beer. Gold.

I lined up glasses on a tray and brought out this silky smooth beer which is named after gold and which people in run-down bars talk about with reverence. For it's not everybody who gets to drink it every day. I started to explain, using the bottle-opener to lay emphasis on my words. There was too much foam on the beer and I didn't go about it very professionally, but my whole mind was on Gunnlöth.

Obviously she wasn't seduced into handing over the mead. That never even came into question!

I said this in a tone of such contempt that the corners of Anna's mouth were pulled down onto her chin. She'd got that dry sarcastic look. Let the others know by her look that she thought I was a little overwrought.

She served him the mead of her own free will! Sitting in the golden chair!

I looked at each of them in turn to assure myself that this information wasn't lost on them. And repeated:

She sat on the golden chair. I just can't tell you how surprised I was when she sat down in the golden chair. When I was so convinced that he was the one sitting in the chair …

I paused in what I was doing and saying, my mind vanishing back into the prison cell at the moment when she approached the chair of gold in her blue-black mantle, so light of foot, so stately, so sure of herself.

That's something Dís *couldn't* have known, I said. And yet she knew it! That feels like a piece of evidence to me.

The cleverest ploy in courtroom dramas, Anna said, deadly serious. The thing only one person knows.

Strange! It was just that the only thing that crossed my mind was that he'd been the one sitting on the golden chair. I mean, even though ... no matter how everything else re-jigged, I felt he had to have been the one sitting there! I can't begin to tell you how idiotic I am!

Then Anna burst out laughing and her husky laughter mingled with the crackle of the crisps she was tipping into a bowl and which she put on the tray next to the beer. Said that we ought to hold a proper banquet. But I wasn't going to let her steal my thunder. I wasn't done speaking. My amazement in the prison cell was so vivid in my mind's eye that I emphasised every word in order to convince these friends of mine how idiotic I'd been (although none of them had in fact contradicted me) – I had to make them understand how idiotic I'd been, this tremendous idiocy when you're blind to what's staring you in the face:

It's true! What earthly reason did I have for thinking that? It was just a wild assumption. I had no reason for believing it rather than the opposite.

And here I had to pause yet again in what I was saying to think, quite forgetting about the bottles of beer in the meantime.

I'll tell you what, I think I must have thought it *logical* that he should have been sitting on the throne, when that's the most completely illogical thing! I feel so *idiotic*! And there I was, sitting with all my assumptions built up into a wall inside my head while she revealed this simple truth to me. Took her seat in the golden chair as if nothing were more natural, so assured of her right to this throne. The goddess herself. If only you could have seen that golden dignity! I can't describe it to you! And then I heard more than a cracking ... I heard a crashing ... it was as if the walls were falling away from my brain in their entirety ... yes, I felt even as if the walls of the prison were falling down ...

I fell silent. I so wanted to be able to put into words what a weight had been lifted from my mind. Or from my brain. They'd been heavy, these walls, when all along I thought I'd been going about with my head held high. And now I felt as if wholesome air was passing freely about my head. I was free of a heavy load, unencumbered like the time I got rid of all those clothes I owned, when one heavy layer after another fell from me ...

How about we drink a toast with this draught of immortality now? Seeing as you've driven the other guests away now as well.

I hadn't even noticed that they'd left.

So much the better, I said to Anna – now you can sit down and take it easy with us.

I took hold of the tray and walked carefully with it over to the table where the Fish and the women were sitting. Saying to them:

Just where, I ask you, where on earth was a sun-goddess meant to sit if not on the golden chair? She who grants life itself ... and immortality ... and how could I ever have imagined she would betray anyone? Here you are, golden beer for you, and for you, and for you. And to Anna as she sat down:

And for you. With compliments of the maitre d'.

They all burst out laughing and we toasted, laughing with happiness, so genuinely close to each other, initiates in the same family joke. They gave off a sincere warmth which gladdened me. I was able to accept it without any difficulty because it seemed natural to me, just as it seemed natural that their joy over my Dís/Gunnlöth should be just as sincere as if she were their own. The look of joy on the face of the little old woman with her head-scarf who was sitting opposite me enfolded me like a crescent-moon because the light in her

183

wonky eyes was directed out into the room on either side of me, although her mouth was smiling at me, and the girl with the curved red lips drawn out onto her cheeks no longer reminded me of a clown. For it's not at all the grimacing mouth that makes people into clowns. It's a sad look in the eyes. She wasn't sad now. And the Fish. What am I to say about him? He filled his chair. His tranquil, floating eyes filled me with a sense of calm and security like before, when he steered me along unfamiliar streets. It was strange to think that these people knew everything about me and that I knew next to nothing about them.

Anna lit a match and held it up to the wick of the red candle. Yes, it had begun to get dark. I hadn't noticed. The grubby curtains blended together with the darkness inside, the street lights not having been turned on yet. No more customers showed up. Nothing happened to break this oneness at the table. It was as if everything and everybody had come to an arrangement to leave us in peace in a cut-off world of our own. And in the dim light of the candle's flame, the table took on a timeless look. We had more beer. Countless images of Dís ran through my mind, bright and beautiful, and yet there was one which grew more insistent than the rest, like a presentiment or a command. It was the image of Dís turning into Gunnlöth turning into the goddess as she had been when she stood firm: *Or else I would be like a broken beaker*. I wanted to be close to her and where else could I seek her out this evening than in the hospital garden where I had sat for God knows how many hours? Where I had pushed her once and for all into the psychiatric assessment.

I got up and left them at the table. Anna had also fallen silent. Sat in thought. Didn't say anything when I said I was going out for a walk. Never barged her way into what other people were thinking. Was just there. No-one else had come into the pub. Strange how few there were this evening. I fetched my coat from the lobby and went out. Walked for a long time along quiet streets until the opening in the hedge, and my feet carried me along familiar gravel paths to the bench by the ash tree … oak tree, I mean.

I sat for a long time and watched the evening's shadows come on. Not a fly could be heard buzzing, nor a squirrel be seen moving. But the breeze brought me the scent of growth from the leaves of the oak tree. It was easy to imagine that I was sitting in a natural clearing some time at the dawn of the world and had never committed any wrong. The rows of trees surrounded me like a seamless blanket of leaves woven in the vegetation's countless different shades, and the brown patches appeared merely to be natural variations in the dusk shadows. What's more, the stagnant pond's steely grey surface was gleaming as if it contained the purest water. For a moment I felt I was sitting in a dream and that when I woke up, everything would be dressed in autumn colours and I knew that it made no difference, because each would lead on from the other in an ever-lasting cycle. When I looked up, the moon was full. No, it had started to wane. The moon here had been dying while Gunnlöth won us all from Hel with her tears. And brought forth the water of life in a golden beaker. I raised my face towards the moon and gulped the spring air down into my lungs … deep down, deep down. *The breast of the one who sips, a holy source of song worked from the life-song of all creation.*

It was mid-morning when I woke up. The whole house was quiet and yet I woke with a start. I had something urgent on my mind. I sat up, gripped by this pressing feeling which your subconscious sets off when it has been active during the night and has something to settle with you. You need to concentrate in order to catch this sort of message and at first I didn't grasp its significance. Was it something I needed to remember? And then it struck me! The question which hadn't been addressed yesterday in my joy and heedlessness but which now brought on a bit of a hangover after the premature festivities. Actually it wasn't a question, but rather a riddle I was unable to interpret. What now? I was at a crossroads and didn't know which way was which. I had no magical ball of twine to follow.

I sprang out of bed and went in my nightdress into the kitchen where Anna was sitting over a cup of coffee.

Anna, – I didn't even start with a good morning, – now, I don't understand –

Just then the phone rang. I snatched up the receiver and couldn't disguise my impatience at being disturbed. The lawyer was on the phone. He asked whether I could come to his office soon after midday. I was so perplexed and intent upon not losing the thread of my thoughts that I didn't even ask him what for. Carried on talking to Anna where I was standing in the kitchen.

There's something odd about this … I need to think … the

thing is that I don't know what happens next. I'm …

I couldn't quite put my finger on it.

Could it be over?

I got myself a cup from the cupboard to give myself chance to catch my breath and poured the hot coffee into it. I suddenly felt intensely hungry and only now remembered that I'd eaten nothing since around midday yesterday except for the crisps. And I tore the end off half a loaf which lay on the breadboard, stuffing it in my mouth without bothering with butter or cheese.

The bread's from yesterday, Anna said, the boy hasn't shown his face yet. And I can't be bothered going out to the bakery.

I sat down across from her at the table. Her frank gaze when she studied me was attentive. She was ready to listen but didn't press me. Her presence calmed me and I felt as so often before that she was the hub of existence, fixed no matter how everything was whirling.

I just don't know how I'm meant to go about this, I said to her. I feel as if I need to do something … say something about this to the lawyer. But I somehow feel it won't make any difference … from a legal standpoint, I mean, whether or not Gunnlöth committed a betrayal.

At a loss, I waited expectantly for Anna's reaction.

She'd lifted the cup half way to her lips but it was as if she were playing with it rather than drinking from it. She held the handle loosely, jiggled the cup so gently that it barely showed and stared down into it with a thoughtful look on her face. Just as if she were reading a fortune. Involuntarily, I stretched forward to look down into the cup. It was half-full of coffee. So if she was telling fortunes, it was from the ripples which formed on the coffee as she jiggled it. She didn't say a word. I have to admit that it filled me with impatience. It was just as if Urthur had come to send me messages with invisible but momentous thought-waves which she meant others to understand without words. Did she mean to give me no answer at all? But of course I should have known from experience that Anna had been weighing up every word, and now all at once she stopped playing with her cup in this way, pushed her chair back so that the floor screeched, then sprawled forwards onto the table, leant on her elbows and ran the fingers of one hand through her hair so that the multicoloured tufts stood up on end. Gazed at me. Her face older than yesterday as is always the way when people are deep in thought.

No, it clearly makes no difference, said Anna, addressing the problem head-on as usual. Sheltering me no more than she usually did.

Then she stretched and sat bolt upright in her chair and the husky voice sounded like a mysterious oracle when she said:

But you can tell him you know who she is now, though, this Gunnlöth.

I flinched. This had such a familiar ring to it. All of a sudden there was a deadly silence in the kitchen, aside from the monotonous buzzing of a bluebottle which affected me like a hypnotic accompaniment to this oracle I was trying to interpret and whose solution was clearly not far off, although it struck me like a bolt of lightning when I remembered the question which was forever beating down on me, ages ago, in some prehistoric period of my life:

Just who was she, this Gunnlöth?

And I had answered:

Odin stole the art of poetic invention from her.

But I had wiped this assertion from my memory. Judged it to be a lie. A ready-made excuse to cover up Gunnlöth's betrayal … could it be? … and yet … it was still getting in my way … I found it hard to think with this buzzing going on.

But he's finished with the mead! The mead is finished!

I rattled this off at Anna like an obsessive half-wit whilst the fly buzzed incessantly inside my head.

Anna frowned and sat for a while in thought. Then she lightened up and suddenly burst out laughing as if the whole thing were wonderful fun:

Listen, it's clearly utter rubbish that he stole the drink. It's no big deal for her to brew up a new lot! That's something I should have seen straight off, a person in my line of work!

Then she pointed an index finger at me, like a teacher with a pupil:

In better bars, the customers steal the glasses. As souvenirs. You must know that!

I stared at her a for moment, open-mouthed, every nerve in my body stretched taut, every muscle tensed until it dawned on me. Of course!

The beaker! He steals the beaker!

Seems likely, doesn't it, Anna answered. Isn't it also because of this beaker that Dís is in prison?

I sprang up from the table. What an amazing idiot I could be! I was no better than Gunnlöth, failing to understand omens and warnings. I was worse. I didn't even understand my own words, couldn't see what was staring me in the face! And yet one clear thought made it through in my mind. I had to get Dís free before the catastrophe happened. I had to prevent it. Save her. Ward off her destiny.

Now my time was in short measure. I was off to the lawyer's at once.

I took a taxi. I told the driver I was in a hurry. It seemed safer to mention it. So that he wouldn't hang around. I thought I could tell from his firm, supple shoulders and middle-aged bald spot that he was one of those taxi-drivers who keep themselves amused behind the wheel in pleasant conversation with ordinary people like myself, about the weather, the spring, and the summer that was on its way, and maybe he'd want to tell me about his summer cottage which he'd started doing up. He took it well and said he'd put his foot down. And didn't talk with me at all the whole way. How could I have been expected to be able to concentrate on the weather up here on the streets of Copenhagen? There were other winds blowing through my mind … another more dangerous Corpse-swallower was circling over me and Gunnlöth. And I had to get the lawyer to understand that now we had to be quick about getting her off before the crime was committed. Now it was a matter of life and death. I needed to be able to put my case in a way that would convince the lawyer.

I knew what Urthur knew, but I was going to act differently. I intended to prevent this. Speak out loud and clear. Not to make do with half-finished verses.

The traffic grew thicker. The driver had to slow down as we were getting near the city centre. He drove into a side-street where the traffic was moving more quickly, then turned into a wider street where the traffic grew heavy again: I didn't know where we were – somewhere near the Canal, I think. Then he slowed down again. I'd become impatient. This was the worst time for it, right after lunch and everybody was hustling and bustling about more than usual. In the end, the driver came to a complete standstill. There was a group of people in front of us walking in the middle of the road. They paid hardly any attention to the cars, acted as if the road was theirs. They covered the pavements too, and they were all heading in the same direction. Could all of these people be coming from lunch? These were clearly ordinary people … I mean, they were people you see serving in shops and banks, who sit in offices … you can tell from the clothes they're wearing … in films they're dressed in skirts and blouses and the men's jackets are slightly creased and when you see them in a group like this the clothing somehow blends together. Where was this swarm of working people off to? The driver said that we'd end up in the middle of the crowd if we carried on. There was obviously some kind of meeting being held here. He was probably right. There was a restlessness in the air. Some were standing with placards and banners and some way off I saw a man jutting up out of the crowd. He must have been standing on something and it was clear from his manner that he was giving a speech. I couldn't make out the words but to be honest I'd had enough. Did we really need to get caught up in an open-air meeting right now, just when I had no time to spare? I had to get going from here at once and asked the driver what direction Strøget was in, telling him that I was going to walk from here on. I paid, and with a bit of skill he was able to get away onto a side street but I had to start elbowing my way forwards through the crowd to make it in the right direction. I took a chance to squeeze my way onwards but the further in I got, the more tightly packed the crowd was. And the people looked different. They were younger … these were teenagers … in colourful tops and jumpers, and jeans for sure … it didn't need any explaining to me … I knew these sort of people through and through. I was barging my way between two young girls holding a banner between them and when they turned aside out of my way the banner was pulled taut right in front of me and cut off my path ahead. On the banner I read: Which would you rather lose: Barsebäck or Copenhagen? I knew that Barsebäck was a nuclear power plant right in the south of Sweden and all of a sudden I felt they'd aimed the question at me, at this woman who was barging her way through … I looked at each of them in turn … two typical teenage girls … just the sort who turn out like this to demonstrate against nuclear power plants. It was just as if I was going to see Dís here with her cascade of fair hair and the blue of her eyes which lets through every feeling …

I had to get a move on … turned on my heel … no time to explain anything or say where I was going even if I'd wanted to … my business was pressing … I tried to alter course in the hope of getting out of the crowd. Squeezed my way through wherever there was a gap to be found, but it was slow going. The people were standing pressed together. They were listening to the speaker, but for me his words ran together. I only made it a few steps forward at a time. All at once I became aware of a commotion up ahead; voices were raised, angry shouts and cries drowned the speaker out. I couldn't see what was happening but before I knew it I got the mass of people in front of me in my arms. The pressure bent me over backwards. I tried to back up and was filled with terror when I wasn't able to move my foot … no space behind me … I had to stand there where I'd ended up … helpless, utterly in the power of this movement which beat against me like a breaker and bent me over backwards … bodies tight up against me … jammed in … I saw right away that it was the police who were pushing people away from them. I no longer had control over my movements. My body was no longer my own, just an indistinguishable part of one big body which swayed back and forth and went on for God knows how far until everything loosened up again and we fell apart from each other, and in a flash – when I felt the solid road under my feet again and could walk a pace of my own free will and sensed I'd become me again – the fear blazed up into such an unbridled rage that I trembled from head to toe. My body like a ball of wool pulled taut, my eyes darting back and forth without me seeing anything until … until I saw Óli. That was surely him over there. He was being jostled and flung back and forth and he didn't have the strength to defend himself. His defencelessness was absolutely appalling. It was then that I was all of a sudden standing behind the wide, black and unwavering back of a policeman as if I was standing up against lifeless stone and I was overwhelmed by my anger over Óli and I clenched my hand as if it were holding a spear, and raised it to strike.

But the man's back, this mute blind back suddenly gained the power of speech; I saw a muscle move slightly, for just a moment, as if hidden inside a stone there was life which was making its presence known. A person's weak spot. Nowhere are you safe from others' vulnerability. I let my arm fall and Óli was carried away like a drop in the ocean, indistinguishable from the others. If it *was* Óli. Maybe it was somebody else.

The crowd began to unravel. The police had left and it didn't look like there was going to be any major confrontation. The commotion had been confined to one area and caused people to start hurrying away. I set off towards Strøget, still a little angry and upset if the truth be told. At the delay as well. To have to get caught up in this now! And why this demonstration in the city centre at such a busy time of day? This is what I was thinking as I walked along and before I knew it I'd arrived on Strøget where calm, ordinary people walked in and out of the shops with merchandise in colourful shopping bags as if nothing had happened there, such a short distance away, by the Canal or wherever it actually was, and then I hurried on to the lawyer, into the part of town with old narrow side-streets overshadowed by the buildings' grey walls. It was as if I'd switched between different worlds at regular intervals on this route which lay behind me.

I shot up the stone steps as quickly as I could. I must really have been late! I was seized all of a sudden by the fear that the lawyer had grown tired of waiting for me and had left. If I got there now to find a locked door! I was so worked up after the day's events that I felt I'd give up without further ado if that happened. Yes, I would sit down on the landing outside his office or just on some street-corner and start bawling. The stone the steps were made of was so hard that it clicked beneath my shoes at every step. The incessant clicks echoed off the stone walls and swished over my head like a whip. I ran before it all the way up to the third floor. Rang the doorbell. Thank heavens! I recognised the sound of his shoes as he shuffled his feet along the floor. Still wearing his sandals.

I flung myself down in the chair to get my breath back. He took a seat at the desk opposite me as usual. I apologised but decided to wait with what I'd come about until I had regained my composure. So that I'd be able to put forward my case in a calm and orderly way. I got my breath back surprisingly quickly and I remember thinking to myself that I didn't seem to be too out of shape physically. Even though I'd not bothered with the least bit of exercise for a very long time. He viewed me with the utmost calm, and then handed me a comb. I couldn't help but smile as I took the comb. My hair must have been in a state for him to be appalled! I told him I'd got caught up in an open-air meeting or some kind of demonstration about nuclear power and he said that something along those lines was to be expected, but of course I didn't get his point and it didn't occur to me that he meant anything in particular; but when I said that it had been a stroke of terrible bad luck or something to that effect but that that wasn't what I'd come to talk with him about (having completely forgotten that he'd invited *me* to meet with *him*), he said:

So you haven't heard the news?

News? What news?

If there was any news about Dís's case then he would have had to tell me it himself. What was the man on about? I thought the question pretty much absurd, general news from the world up here being a far cry from the reality I moved in.

Then he pushed a newspaper towards me with a large headline.

Radioactive cloud over Scandinavia.

That's how I heard about the accident at Chernobyl.

194

He said that little was known as yet. That at first people had thought the radiation came from the nuclear power station at Forsmark in Sweden but that it was known now that the accident had happened at Chernobyl in the Soviet Union three days ago and that the prevailing wind had carried the radioactivity over the Nordic countries.

I felt he was delivering my own death sentence, although of course he couldn't have known that the previous evening I'd been sitting in the garden, gulping down the wind. Oblivious to its message. Oblivious as always! I'd forgotten the language of the winds and air! But that was an absurd thought. All of a sudden I felt it absurd just to think about one person even though that person was myself. Dís ... stuck, becalmed ... to tell the truth I didn't know how I should think in the face of this ... found myself in some sort of vacuum until he said that a lawyer from back home had rung with a request from you.

What? – I said, as if I couldn't work out who he meant. Actually I don't know why I was so surprised. Perhaps because I was forever being jerked between worlds. I couldn't keep up.

Then he told me about your demand for him to request of the Danish authorities that Dís be transported home without delay.

And glancing over at a scrap of paper where clearly he'd scrawled down notes for himself, he went on as if he were reading aloud from the documents.

The demand was to be made on the grounds that it would be irresponsible on the part of the Danish authorities to hold Dís in custody under the circumstances which had arisen and which could have a bearing on her life and well-being, particularly taking into consideration the fact that she was an Icelandic citizen and that it was therefore possible to investigate the case at home and even to pass sentence there. Then you could both go home at once to Iceland, where the prevailing wind was favourable and people were safe from lethal radioactivity.

He looked up from the papers.

Is that possible? – I asked.

It's not an unreasonable demand. It's worth a try of course.

I didn't say anything. Was hesitant all of a sudden. Why? Wasn't trying to get Dís off precisely what I'd come here for? And hadn't I been given the chance to do this? Wasn't this precisely a way of diverting the course of destiny? Of preventing him from stealing the beaker? The journey might break the sequence of events … journey, not retreat … Anna would understand that I wasn't escaping to clean air and untainted water-sources on my own account. She would understand that just such a journey could draw Dís out of Gunnlöth's tale … that getting up out of this prison and forgetting could alter the course of her destiny …

Forgetting?

I got up and walked over to the window.

The white Venetian blinds divided the grey wall of the building opposite into narrow strips. Everything was grey and white. Grey and white. And peaceful. I was very alone. So why didn't I leap at the chance of getting out of this place? I couldn't work it out at first. But there was something which I had not to forget. As sometimes happens when the mind wanders and searches, calling in even on those regions home to death and sickness, I started to have the sensation of my body. Felt that in it there lived a powerful, almost tangible memory of the outdoor meeting when it had become inseparable from the others, when it was merely a cell in a big body whose end was out of sight, my memory being therefore only a fragment of the collective memory of us all, and even if I left, Anna would just wait for the next one who sat down at a red-checked table-cloth in front of a burnt-out candle with its hardened wax. I parted the Venetian blind to see out. Shadows were prowling about the grey wall of the buildings opposite like guardian spirits of evening on its way. The street was deserted. What could have become of Óli? Vanished like Loki who carried inside him the quick of everything which lives because nothing that had once been had ever died off in him … *his games, real life from other times, and his songs memories from other life-spans* … and Gunnlöth who held her head and rocked back and forth as if in dire distress before she was sucked once more into the vortex of the future. Again and again the whirling wheel. All the way up to the end of the world. *Do you want to go on?*

No.

I was calm. Turned around and looked at him. The answer had clearly taken him by surprise. Surprise and enquiry were written all over his face.

We're not going, I said emphatically.

I walked over to him, leaned over the desk in front of him as if I were holding him with my gaze:

He's going to steal the beaker. I want you to request them to stop the psychiatric assessment. Whether you get her off or not. You have to get them to listen to her. You have to convince them that she was reclaiming the beaker. Not stealing it.

I put all my weight into the words which followed. Words welled up out of every nerve, every muscle:

And you've got to do it before it's too late. They have to believe her. The beaker is the hope of life.

I held my breath while he thought over what I'd said. He looked out of the window, turning the side of his face towards me. His ear. The mussel shell. And I tried to convince myself that the rhythm of the ages must surely reside in this ear. Life was now staked on him understanding this. In my quiet concentration I grew optimistic, starting to imagine that he compensated for the dimness of his dingy office with a heightened sense of hearing which enabled him to make out the connectedness of all things – this man had once told me that that he didn't believe in shutting teenagers away in prison and now – now I had to get him on my side. He was sure to see it! He was sure to have an answer! Then he looked at me and said:

Though I would gladly –

I wasn't giving up. I cut in. Put all my weight into the words:

She's telling the truth. That's how it happened. I know. She's not making this up. And she isn't insane.

A trace of sympathy flickered in his face as he looked at me, but I could also see there that he was at a loss and a tiny bit impatient when he began again:

197

You want me to maintain that Dís has actually experienced this at first hand?

You can put it like that as far as I'm concerned.

Admittedly I'm no psychiatrist, but I suspect that it might also be counted as insanity if you experience at first hand the reality of the twentieth century B.C. when you're leading your life in the twentieth century A.D.

Not if time has vanished. Her watch … if all the outward events of the millennia are fake time, but knowledge flows in the blood?

He sighed, almost pained.

If that sort of reasoning were enough to convince others then my profession wouldn't exist. If only it was all that simple!

Simple, he said! Hardly!

I would be laying my own mental health on the line if I were to maintain something like that!

Then I understood the pointlessness of it all. Without uttering another word I made ready to leave. As I opened the door I heard the shuffle of his sandals as if he meant to see me out or stop me from leaving because he called after me:

You mustn't think that I've been sitting idle. I'm going to submit to the court –

No thanks, I said without turning around. I've had enough of the system's reasoning. I place no hope in it.

That's what I said to the lawyer. Had he not been the person he was deep down, he would have asked me if I was firing him. But he didn't. He raised his voice just as I was shutting the door:

So why are you so sure she didn't help him steal the beaker?

I slammed the door behind me.

When I got home it was dark in the pub. I went in by the side door, straight in to Anna's flat. She was sitting in the armchair in the living room by the television, turning it off as I appeared.

Are you ill? – I asked.

No, I've closed for the night. Everybody had left anyway, and no-one else turned up. Everybody's afraid. And people have been advised to stay indoors as well. Might as well just shut up. Sit down and put my pegs up.

She sat with her legs splayed and stretched out full length on the floor in front of her. She didn't ask me anything. I knew she would ask nothing unprompted. I leaned against the door jamb.

I didn't get anywhere, I said. He's going to steal the beaker.

Yes, she answered.

She made no effort to awaken false hope in me. No ready-made words of comfort on her lips. Neither was I expecting any. I tried to put a brave face on it. I kicked off my shoes and hung up my coat on the hook in the lobby. It hung there limply. The sleeves dangled empty and forlorn.

Is it okay with you if I get ready for bed, I called in to her and went into her bedroom to get undressed. Everything seemed to be clinging to me. I hung up my skirt and placed the blouse on top of the jacket which had been hanging there for ages because I always forgot to put it on.

I heard Anna call back:

I came by a dressing gown at some point. If you can find it you should put it on. It's cold.

I couldn't find any dressing gown but there was a woollen shawl at the bottom of the wardrobe and I wrapped it around my shoulders once I had my night-dress on and had got settled down on the couch. I put a cushion behind me and pulled my knees up under my chin. Curled up into a ball. Helped me relax. The curtains were drawn. The only light was the dim glow of the floor lamp in the corner behind the television. Everything was so quiet. I couldn't recall me and Anna ever having sat down like this alone in the living room, just the two of us. Now I almost felt as if we were shut away in silence and isolation after a game that had been lost. Like Dís in prison. It was the same wait.

Anna started taking her socks off. She was moving unusually slowly, massaging her ankles. I was shocked when I saw how swollen they were. But what had I imagined? That she could constantly stand like that serving people without feeling the effects? I got up off the couch, sat in front of her on the floor with my legs stretched out and took her swollen feet in my lap. Gently stroked the ankles and insteps to ease the pain but saw that massaging such swollen feet was no use. I said I'd get a foot bath ready for her and went into the kitchen to get a container.

The mop-bucket's under the sink.

I was so appalled by this that I turned round.

Anna, you don't bathe your feet in a mop-bucket! You must have some other container.

Makes no odds, – and the husky laughter purred in her throat.

I didn't ask what she meant and found a plastic container which I filled with water and brought through. I lifted her feet carefully as if she were crippled and put them in the warm water. It gave me satisfaction to hear her sigh with enjoyment. She seemed to pick up altogether, for out of the blue she said:

Don't you reckon we should have a drop of brandy? The bottle's in the cupboard over there.

When I opened the cupboard and took the brandy out I couldn't help but smile. She always had something new up her sleeve. This person who spent all day around beer so that the smell of it clung to her like an occupational complaint, if she didn't have a five-star cognac stashed away at home! I poured it out, moved a little nesting table up to the armchair for Anna and put her glass there. Now she could take it easy. I curled up again myself in the corner of the couch with my glass. We sipped the brandy and it slipped down with a silky smoothness, but we didn't speak. We didn't even say cheers. We weren't here to have fun. We were waiting because everything had now happened and hadn't yet happened but was still to be allowed to happen because my reasoning wasn't accepted as valid.

Gradually the weariness left me. In the calm and quiet, the day's events began to play on my mind. I felt as if the day had gone on for centuries and that now Anna and I were just trying to last the final stretch. If only the lawyer hadn't let me down. I began to tell Anna about my conversation with him and couldn't master my outrage and contempt when I said:

He even asked how I could be so sure she wouldn't help him steal the beaker!

Yes. Why are you so sure about that?

Anna asked this calmly as if it were the most obvious thing in the world. I turned to look at her so sharply that it was as if she'd jerked my head up by force. I was just as outraged at her question as I had been before. No, even more outraged! That Anna should ask such a thing! Who knew it as well as I did! And confident and unhesitating, I answered:

No-one betrays …

Fell suddenly silent. Didn't finish the sentence. A trace of the irony in Anna's gaze which I know to be precursor to that terrible, unsparing frankness.

You're one to talk.

I closed my eyes. I was calm all of a sudden. So calm that I had to admit that this came as no surprise to me. Deep down I'd been expecting this. And been waiting for it like someone found guilty of a crime who wants to rid himself of his burden. A time of reckoning had now arrived which I had long suspected there could be no turning away from. The moment had come which you have to cope with by yourself, when you aren't allowed to ask for help. The moment when you stand face to face with the wolves.

I got up. Anna had taken her feet out of the foot bath. The water had become cold. I took the tub into the kitchen, poured the old water down the sink and filled the kettle on the stove to heat some more. Waited at the window while it boiled. The only view was of the rubbish bins which I could just make out in the dark, where cats and rats feasted on left-overs when the rubbish wasn't taken away and overflowed. And slowly and sinkingly, I swept up from my mind the facts proving my guilt, even though it made me queasy because the stink of them was so bad.

I was the one who betrayed.

I'd known all along that Gunnlöth was innocent. She was neither seduced by Odin nor in league with him when he stole the art of poetic invention. What had I been saying right from the start: Odin stole the art of poetic invention from her. This is the answer I gave when asked on the spot with no warning. I thought it was an un-thought-out answer. Yes, un-thought-out is exactly what it was! True for that reason. I wasn't on my guard. The truth like a forgotten prisoner inside my mind who saw his chance when the warden's back was turned. And yet I didn't believe what my own voice was saying, requesting before anything else that my daughter be sent for psychiatric assessment. Because my voice resided in the mountain at the land's highest point, and I'd sunk that land when I betrayed Gunnlöth. Didn't speak her language. Forgot how to speak her language.

Since then I've been living in the third land. In a land of guilt. And from there, no-one can hear your voice. Not even yourself. Least of all yourself.

The steam filled the kitchen and misted up the window. The water was bubbling away on the stove. I poured the boiling water from the kettle into the tub and the steam filled my mouth and nostrils and condensed so that it ran in streaks and finally in droplets down my face as I mixed in cold water so that it would be just right as a new foot bath for Anna.

I carried the tub through and the water closed about Anna's swollen feet once more. This time I sat down on the floor. Took my brandy glass and warmed it in the palm of my hand before drinking. Anna was sipping at her brandy too. We didn't say cheers this time round either. There was still one question on my mind.

Why?

I first realised that I'd asked out loud when Anna heaved a sigh and shrugged:

That hardly needs to be asked. They're not exactly kindly regarded, these women who aren't willing to sacrifice everything for love. Just look at this one in the series they're showing on TV at the moment … who wouldn't give the guy what he wanted to know.

Good old Anna! The laughter gushed out of me so unexpectedly that it was as if a dam had burst.

Yes, Anna said – it really makes no difference whichever one you go for.

She spoke as if she had in mind an image of two slices from the same cake!

I wept with laughter until the tears were streaming down my cheeks. Because it struck me as so obvious, and laughter's the only resort when mountains are lifted off your shoulders as if they were feathers. Anna's wisdom was like a well which never ran dry. Yet the laughter died out in a kind of sob, because in reality its source was pain. Or rather the sorrow that stems from the fact that my eyes have become all-seeing, and I can see Gunnlöth where she's shouting out into the night so that her voice rises above the storm and ascends over the lamentation of dying creation: *Or else I would be like a broken beaker* …

Gunnlöth who didn't know betrayal, Gunnlöth who was the goddess who was poetic invention which was love and I sensed her sorrow over the pointlessness of the pain which bites when what belongs together is broken apart.

Anna was still sitting in the room with me when I drifted off into uneasy dreams about a woman in a dark mantle with violet-coloured hair and a violet-coloured scent and feel I know her and yet don't know her until I work out that the woman is myself and I'm holding up a child in my arms who smiles so guilelessly at me that it causes me unbearable pain and all at once I hear a fateful swoosh of wings and I cry out in a deep husky voice: An eagle is flying overhead … an eagle is flying overhead … and wings block out the sun so that it turns dark in the bright of day, pitch-dark, and my mouth and nostrils are filled with the stench of slick wet soil and I see lifeless stones deprived of the goddess's sap and my breathing is laboured, my chest has become the refuge of lizard and snake and I see a destiny heavier than a thousand hearts. The goddess's absence lies heavy over the whole land. And the child at my breast with its nose in my mantle as if it can smell the scent of flowers. I pray to the goddess to take this vision away from me. Until this comes to pass, goddess, I pray to you, never show me this again! I shall do everything in my power to prevent this, but never show me this again!

I released the child from my arms.

I could prevent nothing in spite of my knowledge. Because Dís was on the homeward leg of her trip. She had already lived this even though it still lay ahead. Her narrative was a magical twine of events showing the way, which my vision of the future couldn't alter.

I could draw her out neither from inside the mound nor from the prison cell.

Here in this prison cell we're living in the present what is past and what has yet to come to pass. She carries on into a past which is future.

He rose up from the bed which was reddened with blood like the altar.

He didn't stoop down to her. His eyes neither came to rest on her nor on the signs of the goddess. They were open wide. He raised his arms as if he meant to take flight. Took a deep breath. His ribcage expanded. His long kingly hair fell down onto his shoulders and brought to mind a mane. He was still in the grip of the god's madness, not yet come back to himself, restored and ecstatic after the night's pleasures in the arms of the goddess and couldn't get his bearings. She spoke to him. He looked at her bewildered, without hearing, and she could see that one of his eyes was menacing, the other dim like a dead moon. Still in the power of Niflheimur. She rose up. Touched the eagle's wings to remind him of his exultation and victory over the forces of the beguiling gulf. He drew away like a crazed horse but grew calm when he saw the wings and allowed them to be fastened upon him and then everything happened in the space of a moment but the moment doesn't exist, she said, which would be long enough or short enough for her to be able to grasp what happened and she's never been able to describe it exactly.

In his hand there was something black and heavy which cast such an immediate dimness about the place that it was as if countless suns had been extinguished by a power so heavy with evil that every joint in her body locked, helpless. This was a sorcery she had no control over. At that moment she heard the earth cracking and bellowing with pain and understood then that this was an unearthly object which he had smuggled into the very dwelling of the goddess. It was iron, metal made from premature stone, ripped from the earth's belly, and there would be no escaping the goddess's awful revenge, taken in agony and fury. Earth groaned and thundered. Rocks split apart. With the black, evil piece of smithery, he severed the bars of the clashing crags. Corpse-swallower whines. The sky is smitten with darkness. He has fled through the tunnel. And taken the golden beaker.

The date of Dís's hearing has been decided.

They've given up on the terrorist plot theory. Not least on the basis of a medical certificate. There it states that Dís is far removed from all conception of reality, interacting so inadequately with her environment that she should be regarded as mentally ill and in need of hospital treatment.

And I saw the guilt pass over Dís: I saw the golden sheen of her hair fade and her tresses lose their unruliness and hang dull and lifeless as the boughs of the holy ash thinned out and the leaves fell, one by one, the ones which clung on becoming mottled and withered; I saw her body lose its vigour as the ash's bark cracked because the vital sap was drying up in the holy well – the water from that spring no longer flowed over the land and the channel was empty and dry; I saw the gleam vanish from her eyes as the sun's brightness grew dim and became like a dull-sighted eye and the moon and stars staggered about the firmament like drunkards; I saw the pallor of approaching death pass over her skin as the vegetation was deprived of its strength and the entire landscape became a scorched waste ...

The goddess had forsaken us.

Urthur cautioned me.

Don't forget that you're a priestess. That's what she said to me. But I've failed.

She was forlorn, her eyes sunken with suffering when she asked:

What did I do wrong?

Why didn't Urthur answer? Why didn't she take my Dís in her arms? Why didn't she close the magic circle round this pitiful little body? Wasn't comforting her the only thing to do? But Urthur sees yet further. She knows there's a second oath-breaker about the place.

He swore a ring-oath, Dís said, and in her voice were assurance, amazement and such incredulity that she reminded me of a child who can't understand the things which are taken for granted in the world of grown-ups. She couldn't make it add up. You don't go back on a ring-oath. We smile when children are so naive and urge them to grow up out of such innocence, because having the wool pulled so easily over your eyes is an embarrassment and leaves you vulnerable. And at this moment, my little Dís is wearing Gunnlöth's expression, like a slightly simple child. Oathbreaking is beyond her comprehension. And so she takes the blame on herself. But I found a bit of consolation in it. As long as falsehood is beyond her understanding, there is hope of life and healing.

She is unharmed but betrayed, and most sorrowful of soul is he who is betrayed.

Ages passed while she was speaking:

Urthur was in my lodge in the dark. Everybody else had left. My father and Loki ... What had I done wrong?

Urthur! What have I done wrong?

Urthur stepped out of the dark and laid her hand on my shoulder:

Remember that you're a priestess.

I went down on my knees, my despair so deep that it couldn't be heard. Was Urthur taunting me?

But she remained settled in my lodge. She didn't leave. She didn't foretell my destiny and she didn't break the thread. I didn't know where she had hidden the end but she was in my lodge anyway. I could still sense currents coming from her, sometimes cold, when I huddled myself up like now, and sometimes warm and mild, but most often both at once. I didn't dare speak to her. I didn't know what had become of my relatives and I had no hope that Urthur would tell me anything. I wasn't used to her doing so. But Urthur had changed. Now she told me tidings, sometimes even with great intensity as if it mattered to her that I knew what was happening. And whenever I became downcast with despair, she started speaking.

Odin took the beaker to his royal residence. He declared that the almighty gods had granted him absolute authority over sacrifices and that he alone had knowledge of the gods' will, until some believed that he himself was a powerful god and had power over life and death. To the young warriors – who before had bowed to the goddess and feared Hel's dark visage and the riding of the woman-spirits over the bodies of the slain – he promised eternal battles, and that they might wake up to a new battle, even though they fell among the slain of this world, if they devoted themselves to him.

He incited people to war and conquest and the lakes filled with sacrifices to the war god. The earth is gaping with wounds, men dug up marshes and tore her flesh in their greed for iron, forging weapons from it. Brothers battled. Men were at each others' throats.

And they forgot the goddess, insulted and disgraced her. Her sacred songs they called witchcraft and outlawed. The poets became ornaments for the king's hall.

And Loki?

They put his talent to ill use and bully him about like their dog.

Protect me, Urthur ...

He sent him for the spear.

The spear? Which I myself had hallowed to the goddess the night I last heard of Loki. The spear which only he who had earned the goddess's protection could receive!

I didn't understand.

But Loki was bound to the goddess by his oath, I said.

Two oaths now bind him. Odin needed to make use of his talent and when he saw in Loki's eyes the thirst for ever-new experience and new life he got him in his power. Loki made himself Odin's oath-brother. They mingled blood.

Oh no ... no ... no ...

I covered my eyes even though it was pitch-dark. I wanted to drive from my mind the vision that Urthur had awakened there. I didn't want to see Loki cut the earth-necklace, the holy ring, walk beneath it into the belly of mother earth with Odin and mingle blood with his blood. Reborn as brothers. It was in no mortal man's power to break such an oath. And I knew that Loki's thin and pale skin took a long time to heal.

No, I didn't want to see him, not as he was now. Neither did I want to see the other when he showed up, the oath-breaker who could know no peace. Until now he'd made do with sorcering Urthur into his control, when she lay as if dead while he forced her to tell him his destiny because he is wracked with fear. He can find no peace and trusts no-one, pained and suspicious he fears his oath-brother who will rise against him and the wolf who will devour him, and full of fear he gathers the dead among the ranks of his men because the prophecy is always the same. Urthur knows everything.

He appeared first as a shudder, cold as dead flesh, and then as a shadow darker than the darkness in this place. He skulked like an apparition along the walls with his hood slanting down over his eye, blind from a dull fear, and then Urthur rose up, powerful as she used to be, and her will was directed at me more fiercely than ever before. I didn't understand. What did she want with me? … Remember … yes, but what could I do? … The goddess had vanished and the beaker that was holiest of all objects … but suddenly … the embers in her eyes burned like tongues of flame … and I suddenly remembered and got up off the floor, staggered forwards in the darkness, driven on by Urthur's will which suddenly intensified, and feeling my way, my hand came upon … I thought at first that it was one of the stones of the hall it was so black and invisible … but it was the chest … I opened it and slowly and carefully my hand searched among the decayed tatters of the goddess's clothes until I found the sun-disc. I grasped the handle and hope and fear had me in their grasp as I looked into the disc where the goddess had before been revealed to me … when I stood before her face to face … and I peered into the black surface for a long, long time, oh, what an age before I saw something stirring and coming to life … I saw the brow, eyes, and inside them, the pupils. A face! It was the goddess herself! Come back! And in the blue eyes an indescribable glow which flowed through me as if I were standing in fire. I stood face to face with the goddess … I didn't want to let her go … I held onto her with my gaze … beseeched the one who had turned back not to leave ... and she didn't leave ... she didn't want to leave ... she wanted to enter her residence ... the power of her gaze is bending me ... she's ... she's clearing a path for herself ...

I see her transforming before my eyes. She lifts her slender arms as if she's planning to burst free of these prison walls ... she recognises no limit ... her space is boundless ... she looks up into the sky ... her arms like graceful flying birds in the blue-white haze of the skies. And I become stricken with fear, as the one who shares no part in the revelation – in the grace – always does. I close my eyes, skulk out of the prison.

Over and over again ... cycle after cycle ... I can't bear to experience this one more time ... over and over again in the role of the betrayer.

Over and over again I will condemn this truth to an asylum.

I don't trust myself to be at the trial, I said to Anna.

Is that so?

And there must have been a touch of sarcasm in her reply, for I said:

I'm going to ask the Fish to come with me.

We walked side-by-side up the steps to the courthouse and in through the outer door and had got as far as the lobby which felt spacious to me although I wasn't looking around me. I was thinking about whether they would bring Dís in a police car with a police guard like when they drove her to the hospital for examination by the psychiatrist, and then we walked straight in through a second narrower doorway and into a corridor and my field of vision was constricted even more and if this were in a film I would probably be shown in ever-growing close-up with unnaturally large and slightly distorted features, and I thought that they probably would do because she was still classed as a suspected criminal, although everybody involved knew just as well as I did what the ruling would be. The certificate from the psychiatrist was categorical, and yet she wasn't an ordinary patient. Her illness was a criminal one, and so probably they would do. Bring her in a police car.

The Fish decided where we were to sit and I put my handbag down on the floor. That was all the luggage I had. I didn't want to be weighed down with anything more. I had my airline ticket in my purse. For the extradition had been obtained, although in a revised form. She was to be allowed to serve her sentence at home. Or her therapy. That is, should she be sentenced. They were always saying that, the lawyer and the ambassador who were dealing with the matter. They always tacked this on at the end when they spoke with me. Never forgot to tack it on in order to remind us all that our legal system is a just one. All the preparations had nevertheless been made for a journey home. Should she be sentenced.

The Fish and I waited without speaking. We sat there perfectly still and slightly ceremoniously, probably looking more than anything like guests at a wedding waiting for the bride to be led into church. The moment of destiny. Fate's decree. This is where Urthur had drawn the thread to. This is where she'd hidden its ends. I was calm. Actually I could have drifted away on the slightest of currents. Wouldn't have had the stamina to offer resistance. Because those fated to die are beyond rescue. I was guiltiest of all. I'd got to the end of this treasure hunt.

I felt as if my being there was a formality. Suspense springs from hope. From expectation. And I had no hope. And so I felt as if I wasn't present. Or was just an onlooker. Some people came in. The lawyer. The judge sits down. Fat chance of making a thriller out of this. Even when Dís appeared. Because she had that look on her face which she's had ever since, that free, exulted look. She wasn't present either. Didn't look around her. She didn't seem to be aware that she was before a court. It was just as if she knew that the defendant was sitting somewhere else and my vision dimmed for an instant as if the thoughts behind my eye-lids had turned into raven's wings, and the Crown Prosecutor started speaking. He spoke briefly and it took no effort for me to follow because he said nothing except what I knew he would say. About a defendant who attempted to steal a national treasure. And then the lawyer spoke, and I paid no attention until he started speaking about goddesses.

I was amazed and warmed to the bottom of my heart and yet at the same time I felt for him because I knew that he was laying his own mental health on the line, and he submitted a report from a historian of religion whom he said he'd spoken to, and this expert points to parallels and speaks of a common Indo-European inheritance and says it might be that this is exactly what *Hávamál* is describing if it's examined carefully and he held up a book and to me that seemed fine because

I know that everything twists into its opposite and invention becomes reality and reality invention and so Dís has betrayed neither, but it didn't seem fine to them, and I saw that the lawyer's mental health was under threat because people here only saw things in opposition to each other and had come to bear witness to a schism and to things that couldn't be reconciled and I suddenly gave a start. He asked for the beaker to be brought in. I hadn't been expecting that. The beaker, here! I grasped the Fish's hand. We held hands as a uniformed man came in and placed the beaker on the table in front of the judge. I held my breath. Could see nothing but the beaker. It was like a gilded point of light before my eyes, with whorls which wound like an endless sea-serpent, neither beginning nor ending in it, and everything around me vanished from sight as if I'd only made a brief stop there on the whirling wheel, and my desire and longing and hope were directed at this gilded point of light … my throat grew dry like Gunnlöth's … what was it she said again? … I was gripped by a thirst and didn't know it … but I knew it … I knew I was gripped by this thirst … Dís had stood up and a look had come over the judge as if she were madness incarnate … he was seized for an instant by an anguish which no guards could guard him against … I knew that look … it was the same kind of anguish which used to seize me when confronted with teenagers, and he motioned for the guard to take the beaker out of the room, and when he turned the beaker from his door I knew that this building was a burial chamber, each stone in its walls a stone of cynicism, prejudice and contempt. I knew it from the time when I was like that myself, every cell in my body like the stones in this building. And if you stay in that sort of building, you die, unless you have an inkling of the difference between pitch-darkness and a lightlessness which turns to light which turns once more to lightlessness which turns to light, and I could see Dís's profile when she sat down again like the goddess in the golden chair and took a ladleful from the golden beaker and offered a sip of the water of life so that unsown acres should shoot up and vision should be complete, and the judge's look of relief and the weary forbearance which passed over his face as the lawyer spoke in Dís's defence in open defiance of the medical certificate, and the hope closed up again like wilting meadwort, and the sun lifeless in its throne, and the pale crescent moon stubborn and unbudging in the firmament ... the cycle comes to a halt ... the whirling wheel comes to a halt at this stop in fake time and we both stood up at once, me and the Fish, and I asked in the ice-cold voice of one condemned to die: Is this where I get off?

Ladies and gentlemen. We will shortly be landing at Keflavík airport. Please fasten your seat-belts and remain seated in ...

Christ! Was I standing up? I was completely taken aback! We're landing. I'd forgotten where I was. In a bit of a panic I fumble for my seat-belt and fasten it. Look over at Dís. Need to assure myself that she's got her seat-belt done up. Check on whether they're looking after her, these policemen, although strictly speaking their job is not to see to her safety, but to other people's. To hedge her in so that other people are safe. No, now I'm getting muddled. She's to go into an asylum. Not a prison. She's to be cured of invention.

I've got to pull myself together. Be calm. I look out of the window. We're flying along the coast where the ocean breaks on the rocks and the dwarf birch and the heather on the lava are still so tiny that the eye can't pick them out. The country looks like a wasteland. We've arrived over the airport. Fly over a grey row of fighter-planes in front of a big hangar. Would he get the job now? Seeing as they weren't able to tie Dís to a terrorist group?

We've landed. I grab my handbag. Want to be ready to follow Dís off the plane. Make sure that no-one gets in the queue between us. The first plain-clothes guard stands up, then Dís, and then the other guard, and with a deftness seldom seen he sees to it that I don't get in front of him. Shoves his way in front of me. So perfectly coached is he in dressing his iron will in the disguise of good manners that no-one could accuse him of being impolite and their manner is so humdrum and uninteresting that no-one would imagine they were conducting a crazy person off the plane between them. But I shove my way forwards as well. Need to be near to Dís. Walk close up behind him.

But I don't get far. Two policemen in uniform are waiting when we get off the plane. They too are well-mannered. We are all shown into a side room and we walk there almost as if we were in a parade, Dís and the Danish guards first, and then me with the uniformed men on either side of me.

He's come to meet us. My husband. Dís's father. Stands a little way off. He's looking the men in uniform over, a little uneasy and surprised. Hadn't been expecting this. So had Dís been convicted then, being met as she was by uniformed policemen? Had she not been acquitted? Had she not been found insane, then? Or was giving her this sort of reception just the incivility and confusion of the justice system? Approaches us slowly all the same. His expression perplexed as he stares at me. Doesn't he recognise me? It's as if he's wondering whether it could be me! That's how I remember it. He clearly doesn't recognise me. I'm a woman of three clothes hangers. He's never seen me like this before. The clothes he's familiar with I left behind in Copenhagen. He stops abruptly. Tries to get his bearings. Hasn't a clue what's going on when the guards escort Dís into an ordinary car which is waiting by the door to the street and the uniformed men each take one of my arms and guide me into a police car. He starts, sets off running, stops suddenly and throws up an arm in bewilderment. In the look on his face you can read: this has got to be a misunderstanding! A terrible misunderstanding!

But this is no misunderstanding.

They are arresting me.

I've got the beaker. It's in my handbag.

How did it happen? Well, as the Fish and I were leaving the courtroom, the usher opened the door and let us out. I was numb inside. There was a murmuring in my ears as if my senses were sunk in the depths of the ocean. The Fish walked close by my side and asked nothing. I didn't know where we were going. Neither of us was following the other. We glided along side by side. We walked to the end of the corridor and round the corner. So quiet that nothing could be heard except the unspoken speech between us. Carried on down this corridor and past some closed office doors. They had a troubling effect on me and I slowed down. Stopped, almost. A door on one side was open. I turned my head and looked inside and there it was in front of me on a table. The beaker! I was being shown the unbelievable. There it stood. Up for the taking. For anyone who wanted it. For one who was hungry and thirsty. A national treasure? No, there's neither Dane nor Icelander here, man nor woman and we both set off in the same instant, me and the Fish … there's no need for us to clear a path for ourselves … we're borne by a current … we're following a rhythm which originates somewhere else … somewhere outside ourselves … like two passive drops in an ocean we are carried up onto the crests of the waves and down into the troughs, and our steady breathing is entrancing and isn't disturbed even though I take the beaker and put it in my handbag, and we leave calmly and …

At every step I could have turned back and gone against my current. Against my own rhythm. But I didn't. I took the beaker and was in complete possession of my faculties when I took it. I'll claim nothing else at the trial. So I will be sentenced to time in prison. I couldn't save Dís but I intend to make sure that her truth isn't shut up inside an asylum this time around.

She had a part planned for me ... when she looked at me and made arrangements for me ...

When I'm put into prison I'm going to write down everything that I've thought over on my way through the skies. And may the fish grant you hearing because I'm going to talk our language. Convince all of you that I/Dís/Gunnlöth was reclaiming the beaker. Not stealing it.

I'll begin ... there was something left unfinished ... I still had to finish off the sentence ... no-one betrays ... yes, I'll begin by finishing ... no-one ...

It's a hard one, this part I'm to play.

But no-one betrays their own invention.

The invention which no-one betrays without paying for it with their life. How can that be apprehended?

It's cramped in a prison cell ... the moonlight outside is pale ... and time's passing is measured ...

I have to invoke all things, living and dead, to work the ode which is composed from the life-song of all creation. My words shall be made from the snake's suppleness and the wolf's howl ... the dull glow which gives me light, from the sun's rays ...

And you will see slender hands offering forth the beaker and inviting you to sip of the water of life from a golden source which never dries up as long as you're thirsty ... it's stirring ... the water's stirring ... it's swelling ... it's pouring like a massive wave of song over the brim until a murmuring fills the air ... and at last ... in fire from the prisoner's breast there rises a land.

And then ...

Yes, the trunks of two trees on the shore.

Translator's Afterword

'I don't care what they say on red-letter days about Icelanders' love of literature', Dís's mother tells us with irritation as she recounts her first meeting with the lawyer: 'You don't go poring over the *Edda* on a day-to-day basis.' While it is no doubt true that most Icelanders do not make perusal of their medieval literature a daily habit, *Gunnlöth's Tale* is nonetheless filled with allusions to this older material, allusions that will have far greater resonance with an Icelandic readership than with most readers of English. It seems a good idea, then, to say a few words about this older material: its connection with *Gunnlöth's Tale*, how allusions to it have been dealt with in this translation, and where English versions of it can be found.

The story of Gunnlöth – central to the novel – is known from two sources. The older of these is *Hávamál*, one of a collection of mythological and heroic poems known as the *Elder Edda* (or less commonly, *Sæmundur's Edda*). The more recent source is a thirteenth-century Icelandic treatise for poets: the *Younger Edda*, also known as Snorri's *Edda* after its author, Snorri Sturluson.[1]

As Dís's mother explains after she has visited the library, and dragged 'Snorri and Sæmundur' home with her to Anna's pub, *Hávamál's* telling of the story of Gunnlöth is allusive and hard to interpret. Snorri, on the other hand, while using *Hávamál* as a source, provides an easily accessible and self-contained tale. Dís's mother uses these two sources to retell the story for Anna:

[Odin] did steal the mead, but not from [Gunnlöth]. The mead of poetry belonged to her father Suttungur and he set Gunnlöth to guard over it in a place called Clashing-crags. And he didn't want to give Odin the drink. But she ... hang on a second ... it's in two different books, *Hávamál* and Snorri's *Edda*.

I got hold of Hávamál.

It says here:

Gunnlöth gave me
on a golden chair
a drink of the dear-won mead.

See, she's bringing him the mead there anyway. Or else I don't understand *Hávamál* well enough. It's an ancient poem. Snorri's easier to understand. Look, here's the version I learned. Snorri says: 'Evilworker' – that's an alias, a name Odin went by – 'Evilworker went to where Gunnlöth was and lay with her for three nights and then she let him drink three draughts of the mead.' So you see that ...

Anna nodded.

She let herself be seduced by Odin.

Yes, and that's how he got hold of the mead and made off with it, I said, feeling drained all of a sudden.

At this stage of the novel, Dís's mother is still on the well-trodden path followed by most interpreters of the *Hávamál* stanzas: when the going gets tough with the older text, she falls back on Snorri's explanations, even though the two accounts are not identical in the details they mention. In an interview with Svava Jakobsdóttir published several years after *Gunnlöth's Tale*,[2] the critic Dagný Kristjánsdóttir observes that the portrait painted of Gunnlöth in Snorri's *Edda* is not an especially alluring one: she is a giant's daughter, stupid and over-sexed – easy prey for Odin. Asked whether she had ever accepted this portrait, Svava replies:

No. I was only a schoolgirl when I read the story of the mead of poets for the first time in Snorri, and I didn't believe it. In some inexplicable way I knew that Snorri was wrong. I wouldn't have been able to rationalise it then: it was an emotional reaction, not a rational one. But I went on thinking about Gunnlöth; she stayed with me.

Many years later I began to read myths in a methodical way in order to find out who she was, at which point it seemed obvious to me that in the story of the mead of poets, Snorri had merged distinct myths together. He makes use of *Hávamál*, but doesn't seem to have known or understood the myth or the rites that are depicted in the Gunnlöth episode. The stanzas in *Hávamál* are so grandiose, so impressive, that they must have great meaning. What is that meaning, though?

Later in the novel Dís's mother gains a new and different understanding of Gunnlöth's tale that does not rely on Snorri for explanation. Shortly after *Gunnlöth's Tale*, the author published a scholarly article giving details of her reinterpretation of the *Hávamál* stanzas, the reinterpretation that underpins the novel; this article has since been made available in an English translation.[3]

In the passage printed above where Dís's mother is retelling the tale of Gunnlöth, she quotes explicitly from Snorri and *Hávamál*. As well as such explicit quotations, the novel contains numerous more subtle references to the older material. Motifs and small fragments lifted from the poems word-for-word are worked seamlessly into the novel's fabric; the placement of these fragments in new contexts often suggests a novel interpretation. Making the effect of these references felt in translation is a tricky problem: annotating the relevant passages, for example, seems contrary to the spirit of the book, and risks transmuting what should be a novel into a catalogue of Northern mythology. Instead, existing translations of the *Elder Edda* have been chosen, and where the novel's Icelandic text echoes in some way the text of the older poems, the novel's English text is similarly made to echo the existing English translations of the poetry. This approach does not always come off: in places the wording of the translated poem must be adjusted to maintain consistency within the novel, and some more subtle points are lost altogether. But in most cases, it means that the text of the novel will find the appropriate resonance in the minds of readers who are familiar with the translated poems.[4] Choice of a translation that preserves some of the formal qualities of the poems is important, as alliterative word-pairs in the text of the novel often signal the incorporation of older poetic material.[5] For example: 'You are **G**unnlöth's **g**uest', 'Memory could stop the **wh**irling **wh**eel at any moment...', and 'the **b**lights **b**lasted the one who spoke them'.

Finally, it should be said that familiarity with the older material is by no means a prerequisite for enjoyment of the novel, and it is hoped that the translation is engaging enough that it might encourage readers to seek out further reading, whether it be the mythological material already mentioned, or other work by the author herself.[6]

Endnotes

[1] Yet another pair of names for these two works are the *Prose Edda* and the *Poetic Edda* respectively. English translations of the *Elder Edda* include those of Lee M. Hollander (*The Poetic Edda* (Austin, Texas, 1962)) and Andy Orchard (*The Elder Edda: A Book of Viking Lore* (London, 2011)). An English translation of *Snorri's Edda* is by Anthony Faulkes (*Snorri Sturluson: Edda* (London, 1987)).

[2] Dagný Kristjánsdóttir, 'Hvert einasta orð er mikilvægt: Viðtal við Svövu Jakobsdóttur', *Tímarit Máls og menningar* 51 (1990), pp. 3-13 [cited passage translated by OSW].

[3] Svava Jakobsdóttir, 'Gunnlöð og hinn dýri mjöður', *Skírnir* 162 (1988), pp. 215–245. English translation by Katrina Attwood: 'Gunnlöð and the Precious Mead', in *The Poetic Edda: Essays on Old Norse Mythology*, ed. Paul Acker and Carolyne Larrington (New York, 2002), pp. 27–57.

[4] Some readers might be interested in the sort of thing that has been lost in translation, and so two examples of problematic passages will be mentioned here for the record. On page 45-46 of the translation, Dís's mother is walking in the street after her second visit to the prison, feeling 'as if all the monsters of the night would break free of their fetters and drag me off with them'. Readers familiar with a translation of either the *Elder Edda* or Snorri's *Edda* will recognise the similarities with the Ragnarök passages in those works. Harder to convey in

translation, though, is the full sense of the sentence: '[a car] braked suddenly beside me and a megaphone shot out of the window: Don't forget the meeting … then it was gone'. The Icelandic word for 'megaphone' is *gjallarhorn*; in the old texts, Gjallarhorn is the name of the horn belonging to the god Heimdallur, which he blows to summon the gods to assemble as monsters break loose and the end of the world draws near. This device, which intensifies the atmosphere of the passage with such economy, cannot be transferred to the translation without self-defeating clumsiness.

Another problematic passage is that on page 161 where Odin is led to the entrance of the burial chamber: 'No-one gets inside unless he gives the goddess a ring, because mighty is the tree on which he must be borne before the mysteries open up to him.' The Icelandic text is a paraphrase of a stanza from *Hávamál*, but one which provides a novel interpretation of that text. In other translations and commentaries, the word rendered here as 'tree' is taken to mean the wooden bar on a door, and the stanza is construed as a warning against over-generosity (Orchard gives: 'It's a stout beam that must be swung | to grant an entrance to all'). In *Gunnlöth's Tale*, 'tree' is made to refer to the ash on which Odin is hung. The allusion is a hard one to deal with because the traffic between the text of the novel and that of the poem goes both ways: allusions to poems affect our reading of the novel, but at the same time, in the text of the novel Svava offers new ideas on how those old poems might be reinterpreted. Consequently, there is no existing English translation of the passage that at all reflects Svava's paraphrase of it, and the reader will not recognise a reference to *Hávamál* here no matter which translation they are familiar with.

[5] To this end, Orchard's translation (see note 1) has been used where possible, with recourse to Hollander's where the desired metrical devices are lacking.

[6] One other book of Svava Jakobsdóttir's fiction has been published in English: Svava Jakobsdóttir, *The Lodger and Other Stories*, trans. Julian Meldon D'Arcy, Dennis Auburn Hill and Alan Boucher (Reykjavík, 2001).

SELMA LAGERLÖF

Lord Arne's Silver
(translated by Sarah Death)
ISBN 9781870041904
UK £9.95
(Paperback)

The Phantom Carriage
(translated by Peter Graves)
ISBN 9781870041911
UK £11.95
(Paperback)

The Löwensköld Ring
(translated by Linda Schenk)
ISBN 9781870041928
UK £9.95
(Paperback)

Selma Lagerlöf (1858-1940) quickly established herself as a major author of novels and short stories, and her work has been translated into close to 50 languages. Most of the translations into English were made soon after the publication of the original Swedish texts and have long been out of date. 'Lagerlöf in English' provides English-language readers with high-quality new translations of a selection of the Nobel Laureate's most important texts.

VICTORIA BENEDICTSSON

Money

(translated by Sarah Death)

Victoria Benedictsson published Money, her first novel, in 1885. Set in rural southern Sweden where the author lived, it follows the fortunes of Selma Berg, a girl whose fate has much in common with that of Madame Bovary and Ibsen's Nora. The gifted young Selma is forced to give up her dreams of going to art school when her uncle persuades her to marry, at the age of sixteen, a rich older squire. Profoundly shocked by her wedding night and by the mercenary nature of the marriage transaction, she finds herself trapped in a life of idle luxury. She finds solace in her friendship with her cousin and old sparring partner Richard; but as their mutual regard threatens to blossom into passion, she draws back from committing adultery and from the force of her own sexuality. The naturalism and implicit feminism of Money place it firmly within the radical literary movement of the 1880s known as Scandinavia's Modern Breakthrough. Benedictsson became briefly a member of that movement, but her difficult personal life and her struggles to achieve success as a writer led to her suicide only three years later.

ISBN 9781870041850
UK £9.95
(Paperback, 200 pages)

HENRY PARLAND

To Pieces

(translated by Dinah Cannell)

To Pieces is Henry Parland's (1908-1930) only novel, published posthumously after his death from scarlet fever. Ostensibly the story of an unhappy love affair, the book is an evocative reflection upon the Jazz Age in Prohibition Helsinki. Parland was profoundly influenced by Proust's *À la recherche du temps perdu*, and reveals his narrative through fragments of memory, drawing on his fascination with photography, cinema, jazz, fashion and advertisements. Parland was the product of a cosmopolitan age: his German-speaking Russian parents left St Petersburg to escape political turmoil, only to become caught up in Finland's own civil war – Parland first learned Swedish at the age of fourteen. To remove Parland from a bohemian and financially ruinous life in Helsinki, his parents sent him to Kaunas in Lithuania, where he absorbed the theories of the Russian Formalists. *To Pieces* became the focus of renewed interest following the publication of a definitive critical edition in 2005, and has since been published to great acclaim in German, French and Russian translation.

ISBN 9781870041874
UK £9.95
(Paperback, 120 pages)